Her face lit with enthusiasm, Dr. Estelle Decker said, "Ah! Josetta Wilson. Very interesting. This is not your typical suicide bomber. She didn't freely volunteer, she was manipulated."

"With drugs?" I asked.

"Possibly, but there are other strategies. I'm going to show you how to brainwash susceptible subjects."

"What makes them particularly susceptible?"

"Good question," said Estelle with an approving nod. "Susceptible people are followers, joiners. They seek the answers outside themselves. They long to belong to something greater than they are, where they'll find meaning and direction for their lives. They are waiting to be molded, changed."

"So a strong self-image and a feeling you are master of your own fate inoculates you against brainwashing?" I asked.

Estelle shook her head. "Not necessarily. Even people actively resisting can succumb, given the right circumstances."

"Even me?"

She gave me a wolfish grin. "Even you."

Visit

Bella Books

at

BellaBooks.com

or call our toll-free number

1-800-729-4992

Death by Death

A Denise Cleever Thriller

Claire McNab

Bella
BOOKS

2003

Copyright© 2003 by Claire McNab

Bella Books, Inc.
P.O. Box 10543
Tallahassee, FL 32302

Printed in the United States of America on acid-free paper
First Edition

Editor: Anna Chinappi
Cover designer: Bonnie Liss (Phoenix Graphics)

ISBN 1-931513-34-1

For Sheila

ACKNOWLEDGMENTS

My deepest thanks to my editor, Anna Chinappi; proofreader Pamela Berard; and typesetter Therese Szymanski.

ABOUT THE AUTHOR

CLAIRE MCNAB is the author of fifteen Detective Inspector Carol Ashton mysteries: *Lessons in Murder, Fatal Reunion, Death Down Under, Cop Out, Dead Certain, Body Guard, Double Bluff, Inner Circle, Chain Letter, Past Due, Set Up, Under Suspicion, Death Club, Accidental Murder* and *Blood Link*. She has written two romances, *Under the Southern Cross* and *Silent Heart*, and has co-authored a self-help book, *The Loving Lesbian*, with Sharon Gedan. She is the author of four Denise Cleever thrillers, *Murder Undercover, Death Understood, Out of Sight*, and *Recognition Factor*.

An Australian now living permanently in Los Angeles, she teaches fiction writing in the UCLA Extension Writers' Program. She makes it a point to return once a year to Australia to refresh her Aussie accent.

PROLOG

It is all unfolding, like a waking dream, like fate. Everything is as it should be, as has been foretold. She tingles with anticipation. She is blessed, she is the chosen one, correctly moving through the singing slices of time in their exquisite order.

The crowds part before her, as has been prefigured. People are laughing and talking, eating and drinking—unknowing celebrants at a consummation soon to be made complete and perfect.

Her spirit leaves her body to watch her physical self walking the black line, invisible to others, that she must tread. Her loose clothing flows gracefully as she paces the foreordained steps. Her long, brown hair is lustrous in the glare of the lights the television crew has set up.

She sees herself smile as Senator Jonathan O'Neven enters, confidently striding along his own predestined path. He doesn't look down, but surely he can see stretching ahead of him the thick black line that intersects with hers on the raised platform, at the exact point where a speaker's desk, sprouting a forest of microphones, has been set up.

Around her people cheer and clap. Some call out his name. She joins their acclamation. It is right and proper to do so. The moment is at hand.

"My friends . . ." he says, throwing wide his arms. The room becomes quiet.

Relief suffuses her. She hasn't failed the task. She is sanctified, set apart, ordained. Putting her hand through a slit cut in her clothing, she hooks her forefinger through the waiting metal loop.

She mounts the two steps to the platform. Someone moves to stop her, but she evades him. Senator O'Neven is staring at her, surprised.

She flings her free arm around his neck. "I am come to you," she says.

Her finger tightens. The ritual is complete.

CHAPTER ONE

The photograph had frozen Dr. Graeme Thorwell in mid-smile. He had a truly dazzling set of very white teeth, contrasting nicely with his tanned face. His hair was thick, dark, and grew to a distinct widow's peak. His blue eyes crinkled at the corners, the line of his strong jaw caught the light, showing taut, healthy skin. He had broad shoulders, a flat stomach, and an excellent taste in casual, expensive clothes.

"He's a beauty," I said. "How much is genuine?"

Dr. Peter Reynolds, ASIO expert in all things psychological, and as homely as Graeme Thorwell was handsome, flicked another photo across his desk. "Your cynicism does you proud, Denise," he said, grinning. "In your hand is the *after*. Now behold the *before*."

It was clearly the same man, if one disregarded the bat ears, the muddy eyes, the crooked teeth. The strong, dark hair was identical, as were the broad shoulders. But in this photograph the subject had a soft belly, a shapeless nose, and an ill-defined jaw line.

"Wow," I said. Bring me that plastic surgeon! If he can do *this* much for Thorwell, what could he do for me?

"Don't fish for compliments, kiddo," Peter admonished. He passed me another photo. "This is Graeme Thorwell in transition."

The ears were pinned back, a cosmetic dentist had been paid a small fortune, and a personal trainer—possibly aided by a little judicious liposuction—was well on the way to tightening up the body and getting rid of the incipient paunch. Thorwell's undefined nose still needed to change, and his eyes lacked blue contact lenses. And at this point of his transformation, his choice of clothing indicated no sense of style whatsoever.

Frowning at his untidy desk, Peter said, "I've got a detailed bio of the guy somewhere."

His desk was crowded with framed photographs of his family— wife Stephanie and four children—taken at various ages over the years. Peter himself beamed from many of the pictures like the proud father he was. Intensely competitive in all things, he'd tried to imbue his children with the same philosophy. This meant Peter was to be avoided on Mondays, when he would insist on recounting in paralyzing detail the latest weekend sporting exploits of his offspring to anyone unfortunate enough to provide an audience. It was Monday today, and I'd already endured his narrative about the achievements of Fanny at softball, Sophia at gymnastics and Pierre at tennis. Happily Baby Jake was too young to play any organized sport, although Peter confided he was convinced Jake was showing early signs of superior hand-eye coordination.

After much rustling, Peter exclaimed, "Here it is!" Handing me the manila folder, he said, "Let me give you the short version of Graeme Thorwell's life. He was born in Chicago, the only son of middle class parents. The family was comfortably off, but even so it was helpful that Thorwell was very bright, and so had little trouble gaining scholarships for his education. He was studying medicine when his adored younger sister died of heart failure related to anorexia. She literally starved herself to death. That tragedy impelled Thorwell to go into psychiatry, specializing in the problems of adolescent girls and young women. He became an authority in the area of anorexia and bulimia. Later he branched off into treating young people rescued from cults. Within his own circle he'd gained a reputation for innovative, effective treatments."

"He was a rough diamond, ready to be polished?"

Peter grinned. "Exactly. Professionally Thorwell was very successful, but he lacked the style required to be psychiatrist to the stars. Then he met the excessively rich Fenella van Berg."

"A sexual relationship?" I asked.

"The woman's as ugly as I am," said Peter with a sardonic smile, "but money does make you attractive, and the more money, the more beautiful you become."

Fenella van Berg's name was familiar to me. She was a staple of the celebrity magazines, being so famous as to only require her first name as identification. She'd been in her early twenties when she'd inherited several billions from a Texas oil father, who had achieved a spectacular death on Mount Blanc whilst attempting to circumnavigate the globe in a hot-air balloon.

Fenella's square, solid body and coarse-featured face had not dissuaded a fading movie icon from declaring his undying love for her. He'd been the first of her three unfortunate excursions into matrimony. Two she'd divorced, pre-nuptial agreements ensuring they only got millions, not billions. Her third husband, a lower echelon British pop singer fifteen years younger, had recently managed to kill himself with an overdose of cocaine and speed while cavorting with groupies in a hot tub.

"I haven't noticed Dr. Thorwell and Fenella as a hot gossip item. Is he planning to be spouse number four?"

"Thorwell has a far greater importance to her than prospective husband material." Peter leaned over to pass me another photograph. "This is Fenella and her daughter, Rosemary, taken last year."

Fenella van Berg's only child was the offspring of her second marriage to Australian Rafe Lloyd, a sculptor who had preferred to live an artistic life without actually having the inconvenience of producing any works of art.

It was clearly a paparazzi photograph. Mother and daughter had been caught exiting a limousine. Fenella's face was clenched in a ferocious scowl. Her daughter, skeletally thin, had half-turned her head away.

"Neither of them appear happy," I said. "In fact, the daughter looks positively morose."

"As well she might," said Peter. "Rosemary has been diagnosed at various times as anorexic, bulimic, bipolar and schizophrenic. She's been in and out of various clinics and treatment protocols in the States, in Europe, and here in Australia. She's made three documented suicide attempts. Not a happy young woman."

"So this is where Graeme Thorwell comes in?"

"Exactly. It just so happens that Dr. Thorwell is the only psychiatrist who's been able to get through to Rosemary Lloyd in any meaningful way. That was enough to win Fenella's heartfelt gratitude."

I looked again at the before and after photos of the doctor. "Appreciation that led to Thorwell's remarkable makeover?"

"That, and much, much more. She's financed exclusive clinics devoted to the treatment of young women with mental or emotional problems, and she's put Graeme Thorwell in charge." He grinned at me. "Oh, to have almost unlimited funds! Because her beloved Rosemary chooses to wander between the United States, Europe and Australia, her mother has established clinics in each location. The European one is outside Paris, in the States it's Houston, and here in Australia, the clinic, rather sickeningly named Easehaven, is located on the Central Coast of New South Wales."

"And what continent is Rosemary on now?"

"Here in Australia, the land of her birth. Fenella van Berg's in New York, but resting easy, because Graeme Thorwell is here to keep an eye on her daughter. In fact, although she's not officially a patient, Rosemary's staying at Easehaven under Thorwell's care."

6

I'd just had a delightful vacation in the Caribbean, and this was my first day back at work in Canberra. It was also day one of my training for my next undercover role, and Cynthia, my ASIO control, had already given me a sketchy idea of what the assignment involved.

ASIO—Australian Security Intelligence Organization—was responsible for internal security within Australia, and worked closely with its foreign counterparts. A month ago a suicide bomber had detonated a device that had killed both herself and visiting U.S. Senator Jonathan O'Neven at a social event held by the Australia-America Friendship Alliance, a non-partisan group dedicated to strengthening ties between the two countries. The CIA had immediately become involved with the investigation.

The media had been told the young woman had been linked to Al Qaeda, although so far there was no firm information as to her identity. Neither of these statements was true.

For political reasons, it suited both the Australian and United States governments to lay the blame at the feet of the Al Qaeda terrorist organization, but unfortunately the most strenuous efforts by the intelligence community had been unable to turn up any evidence of this.

And the suicide bomber's identity had been established. After television footage of the assassination had been compared with photographs of young women reported missing, the best match had been for nineteen-year-old Josetta Wilson, a British citizen, whose frantic parents in London had reported they were unable to locate their daughter since she'd checked herself out of Graeme Thorwell's Easehaven clinic, where she was being treated for depression.

Subsequent DNA testing had confirmed Josetta Wilson had indeed been the assassin, although where she obtained the materials and know-how to make the bomb remained a mystery.

Josetta had left nothing behind to explain her motivations. For reasons entirely unknown she'd decided to blow herself and Senator O'Neven into the next dimension.

"I think I should tell you," I said, "that I know about Josetta Wilson." I had to smile at his chagrin. "No, Peter, I'm not psychic. Cynthia told me."

"Blast Cynthia," he said, with a reluctant grin. "I was about to whip the Josetta rabbit out of the hat. Cynthia's ruined the moment." He frowned at me in mock irritation. "And I suppose she's blabbed about Anita Hutching too."

"Who's Anita Hutching?"

Peter looked pleased. "I didn't think the info would have filtered through to Cynthia yet. I only found out a couple of hours ago, myself. Do you remember Bea and Danny Kern?"

"Vaguely. They had something to do with the Wilton bankruptcy scandal, didn't they?"

"That's right. Douglas Wilton was accused of embezzling millions of dollars from his company before declaring bankruptcy. The Kerns were the company accountants, and knew where the bodies were buried. They were set to testify against Wilton when they were killed in a head-on crash. Without them, the case fell through."

"There's a connection to Graeme Thorwell?"

"There is. Witnesses said the young woman driving the vehicle that veered over to the wrong side of the road and crashed into Bea and Danny Kerns' car appeared to do so deliberately. It wasn't an accident. She couldn't be questioned because she died at the scene. Her name was Anita Hutching, and she had been a patient staying at a certain clinic."

"Easehaven Clinic, by any chance?"

"You're not just a pretty face, Denise. Anita Hutching had been a patient of a Dr. Norah Bradley, who gave evidence at the inquest that Anita Hutching was being treated for severe depression and had attempted suicide on more than one occasion. What was not mentioned at the inquest was that Dr. Bradley worked for Graeme Thorwell at Easehaven Clinic."

"So?" I said. "The clinic's whole *raison d'etre* is to treat emotionally and mentally disturbed people. It isn't so far-fetched to imagine two of the patients could be involved in suicidal violence."

8

"Not on the face of it," said Peter, "unless you take into account the interesting fact that a patient at Thorwell's Paris clinic stabbed a leading French intellectual to death, then ritually disemboweled herself."

"Killer women," I said, shaking my head. "And we're supposed to be the gentler sex."

"*Supposed* to be," said Peter. "Did I tell you about Fanny at the softball match on Saturday?"

"You did," I said quickly. To change the subject before he launched on his children's sporting feats again, I went on, "Cynthia tells me our CIA friends are fully involved."

I was using the term *friends* with an ironic twist. Although ASIO and the CIA, plus all the other alphabetic organizations in the various intelligence arms of our two countries, were pledged to fully cooperate with each other, in practice there was often more rivalry and point-scoring than collaboration.

Peter gave a disgusted grunt. "Unilaterally those CIA bastards put a woman agent undercover into Easehaven as a manic-depressive patient. We knew nothing about it until a week or so ago."

"If someone's already in place, why put me undercover as well?"

"The operative reported there was an undisclosed treatment unit in the high security section of the clinic that seemed very suspicious. Other than that, the information the CIA was getting out was of poor quality. Now it's dried up altogether."

My skin prickled. I'd been in dangerous undercover situations often enough to feel an empathetic chill. "Is the agent all right?"

"When her fictional parents called from the States to check on her progress, they were told she was under sedation because she'd threatened to hurt herself and other patients."

"Thorwell's stumbled to the fact she's a CIA plant?"

"Not necessarily. It isn't morally right, but many institutions sedate individuals for reasons other than medical. People who are troublemakers, who question their treatment, disturb other patients . . . It's easier to keep them quiet than to cope with the disruption. Maybe she made a fuss, as part of her act, and they tranquilized her as a matter of course. The CIA have agreed to brief you. It's possible you'll be asked to help extract her, if necessary."

"If I'm going undercover as a patient of Dr. Thorwell's," I said, "you can forget about giving me anorexia nervosa as my disease du jour." I stood, arms spread. "Look at this body. I may be fit, but no one would call me sylphlike."

"True. You don't have that interesting emaciated look about you."

"If anorexia is off, how about phobias? I do phobias well. You've no idea what I can be scared of, if I try."

Peter laughed. "It's a pity, but your skills in that direction will not be required."

"No? I'm quite disappointed. I was planning pathological fear of germs. That's always a good one, with lots of hand washing and recoiling from dirty surfaces."

"We have something a little more challenging in mind."

The amusement in his voice made me look at him suspiciously. "How challenging?"

"It'll require quite a bit of preparation on your part."

This was par for the course. I'd had to do in-depth preparation into the fictional backgrounds of all my undercover personas. "If I'm not a patient, who am I? A business manager? An efficiency expert?"

"A person highly recommended by Fenella van Berg herself. There's no way Dr. Thorwell will fail to welcome you with open arms. His benefactor speaks, and he obeys."

"Oh come on!" I said, grinning. "Don't keep it a secret."

Peter made a grand gesture in my direction. "Denise Cleever, meet Dr. Constance Sommers, respected psychotherapist."

"You're kidding me! A psychotherapist?"

"Don't worry," he said soothingly, "I'm here to give you a crash course in everything you need to know."

"I can handle it already," I said. "I know the drill. All I have to say is: *And how does that make you feel?* at regular intervals. Simple, really!"

CHAPTER TWO

"Dr. Graeme Bruce Thorwell," said Estelle Decker, "has shown keen interest in rehabilitating young people who have been sucked into the maws of various cults." She gave me an acid smile. "I was present at an address Thorwell gave to mental health professionals where he called himself a cult-washer, and, pity help me, a rescuer of young souls, thus exhibiting the hubris typical of his ilk."

"His ilk being?"

"Any professional who thinks of himself or herself as a savior. You do what you can, use the latest drugs and techniques, and hope for the best. No easy answers. What works with one patient won't necessarily work with another."

Estelle Decker, a brilliant psychiatrist herself, also functioned as a consultant to ASIO, as well as other government bodies. She was an acknowledged international authority on the psychology of persuasion and conversion techniques—in short, brainwashing.

Comfortably plump and wearing loose clothing and comfortable shoes, Estelle appeared a rather vague, pleasant, set-in-her-ways, grandmotherly type. People took her at face value at their peril. In actuality she had a steel-trap brain, a ribald sense of humor and a total lack of patience with anyone or anything she termed wishy-washy.

She worked out of her home, a rambling old house in a leafy northern suburb of Sydney. This morning I'd flown up from Canberra with Peter Reynolds. Later, Peter and I were to meet at the hospital where Senator O'Neven's surviving bodyguard was being treated, but first I was spending several hours with Estelle learning more about Graeme Thorwell.

She ushered me into what she called her "thinking room." This turned out to be a cross between a study and a recreation area. A large flat screen TV took up half of one wall, and French doors, looking out onto a tree-filled back yard, took up a fair portion of another. All other wall space was lined with shelves on which were crammed books, papers, folders, video tapes, DVDs and assorted strange, unidentifiable objects. A computer sat on a battered desk, together with two printers and a fax machine. Fully a third of the floor area was taken up by a billiard table with splendid carved legs. A stationary bicycle was crammed against it. An ancient coffee per-colator hissed and wheezed on a small table that also held an assort-ment of mugs, some of which had pens, pencils, screwdrivers, scissors and highlighters shoved into them.

I leaned back in the embrace of an old leather lounge chair, pulled up my feet to sit cross-legged, and said, "Tell me more about Graeme Thorwell."

"All in good time." Estelle poured two cups of thick black coffee. "If you like sugar or milk, you're out of luck," she said, handing me one.

Sinking into a chair opposite mine, she said, "There's a rumor going around you're thinking of leaving ASIO."

"Where did you hear that?"

Estelle's lips quirked. "I'm not a woman to reveal my sources. Is it true? If so, it's a pity. You're very good at what you do, even if you are dangerously impetuous at times."

For Estelle to say I was good at my job was high praise indeed. I took a sip of my coffee—it was a cousin to hot tar—and said, "I thought seriously about taking a job outside, but decided against it."

"Why?"

I didn't answer straight away. When I received an offer of a better-paying, private intelligence position, what really had decided me not to leave the grandly named Australian Security Intelligence Organization? "Don't laugh at me," I said at last, "but it boiled down to patriotism. I love my country."

"Good answer." Estelle took a substantial gulp of her coffee, smacked her lips as though it actually tasted okay, and got down to business. "Graeme Thorwell specializes in the treatment of suggestible young women, using drugs, hypnotism, and various psychological techniques that can be lumped together under the popular term of brainwashing. Not one of the strategies he uses is illegal, or even unethical. However, he may have crossed the line with some of his patients."

"Deliberately?"

"That's what you're going to find out, my dear."

"I know you've met him professionally. What do you think of him as a person?"

"Needy."

I blinked at her in surprise. This wasn't what I was expecting. "Needy? Thorwell's got good looks, however he obtained them, and status in his profession. I don't think he's poor, either. By anyone's standards, he's a success."

Estelle spread her hands. "You asked my opinion. I gave it. As a child, Graeme Thorwell had a very demanding, harsh father, who required his son's superior performance in all things sporting or intellectual. Young Graeme obliged, but underneath it left him with a hunger for approval. He needs to be appreciated, praised. At the same time, he likes to be in control, to have power over people's lives." She gave a snort. "He's chosen the perfect profession for that. We psychiatrists spend a lot of time with patients who are deeply dependent on us. Bad for one's character, in the long term."

"Has it ruined your character?" I inquired.

Estelle gave a cackle of laughter. "Absolutely. I'm a tyrant, a despot. Haven't you heard that?"

I grinned at her. "Often, but I've always discounted it."

She laughed some more, then abruptly sobered. "Okay, let's move on. First, a fast profile of your typical suicide bomber. These people are not wide-eyed crazies, even though it might seem so, since they willingly volunteer to die. Psychological tests of would-be bombers, who failed for one reason or another to trigger the charges strapped to their bodies, show them as being normal, whatever that word might mean."

"But they're fanatics, right?"

"One can be a fanatic without being clinically insane, my dear. Otherwise a deeply religious person driven to convert others, or an environmental activist, or indeed anyone holding extreme views about anything, could be labeled mad, bad and dangerous to know."

I gave her a cheeky grin. "Mad, bad and dangerous to know could describe you."

Estelle looked pleased. "I take that as a compliment."

"Do these psychological tests of failed bombers show anything useful?" I asked.

"They're mostly young adults who volunteer to be human bombs, rejoicing in the knowledge they will be honored as martyrs. Their personal history frequently shows timidity, introversion. They have trouble showing feelings. When they take this role that asks them to sacrifice their lives, they see themselves becoming icons, heroes of their culture. Fear of death doesn't seem to enter into it. It's something larger than they are, something more glorious."

"So these suicide bombers are not brainwashed?"

Estelle shook her head. "Immersed in a culture that worships martyrdom, perhaps, but not brainwashed."

14

"So how do you account for Josetta Wilson? She didn't come from a culture that worshipped martyrdom. She was born in London into a standard, middle-class family. No fanatics, not even one batty relative—just ordinary, salt-of-the-earth people."

Her face lit with enthusiasm, Estelle said, "Ah! Josetta Wilson. *Very* interesting. This is not your typical suicide bomber. She didn't freely volunteer, she was manipulated."

"With drugs?" What remained of Josetta Wilson had been tested for chemical substances, but nothing had been found.

"Possibly, but there are other strategies. I'm going to show you how to brainwash susceptible subjects."

"What makes them particularly susceptible?"

"Good question," said Estelle with an approving nod. "Susceptible people are followers, joiners. They seek the answers outside themselves. They long to belong to something greater than they are, where they'll find meaning and direction for their lives. They are waiting to be molded, changed."

"So a strong self-image and a feeling you are master of your own fate inoculates you against brainwashing?"

"Not necessarily. Even people actively resisting can succumb, given the right circumstances."

"Even me?"

She gave me a wolfish grin. "Even you."

I found that hard to believe, but wasn't going to argue with a notable authority on the subject.

"As you know, the polite way to describe brainwashing is to use the mild term, conversion techniques," Estelle said.

"Conversion techniques sounds vaguely religious to me," I remarked.

"As well it might. Revivalist meetings in the eighteenth century laid the groundwork for modern manipulation of people's minds. Conversion techniques are designed to wipe the brain clean, so it becomes a blank slate ready to accept new programming. Hence the term brainwashing."

"So how do you get a blank slate between the ears?"

"A good place to start would be to look at the classic brainwashing methods used by cult leaders such as David Koresh or Jim Jones. How do they convert ordinary people into wide-eyed extremists willing to die for their beliefs?"

"Formidable persuasion, I imagine."

"It's alarmingly simple. Let's say you have a normal, commonplace guy called John Smith. One way or another, he gets sucked into attending a cult meeting, although, of course, the word cult is never mentioned. So now he's in a group-think situation where each person is encouraged to feel part of a greater whole."

"Does there have to be a majority of believers in this group for it to work?"

"Amazingly, there doesn't need to be *any* believers, Denise. The charismatic leader enters and becomes the focus of everyone's attention. John Smith is mildly curious, perhaps. He finds he's not to speak or move or do anything to disturb the concentration of the group. The leader begins to work on the emotions of the audience, using every skill of oratory, argument, and psychological manipulation available. John Smith gets swept up in the intense feelings of fear, excitement or anger that crackle through the room. The tension's ratcheted up. The leader becomes more and more passionate. Now the tension is close to unbearable. No one is permitted to leave, no matter how urgent the need."

"What if John Smith has to go to the bathroom?" I asked.

Estelle grinned. "That's too bad for Mr. Smith, and a plus for the cult leader, as Smith's discomfort adds appreciably to his anxiety level. The longer the intense, stressful feelings are maintained, the more John Smith's ability to make sound judgments is impaired. He feels his head will burst. There seems to be no end, no release from this intolerable tension. Psychological overload occurs. John Smith and most, if not all of the group, break down and submit to what they perceive as a higher power. Their brains are wiped clean of former beliefs, attitudes and values." She clapped her hands with every evidence of delight. "Reprogramming can begin."

"But once John Smith's out of that room, won't a good talking to from a friend set him straight?"

"I wish," said Estelle. "It's typical to find those who have gone through such a conversion will vehemently insist that they have not been brainwashed, but have had the essential truth revealed to them."

"So I couldn't talk John Smith out of it?"

She shook her head. "Very unlikely. What you have to do is re-wash his brain, and reprogram it the way it was before."

"You make it sound like we're all programmed, one way or another."

"Yes," said Estelle. "I do, don't I?"

Guarded 24-7, Chip Foster lay in a stark hospital room, the upper half of his face, including his eyes, covered by dressings. One hand was heavily bandaged and he wore a cast on the other arm.

As one of the two men protecting Jonathan O'Neven during public appearances on his Australian tour, Foster had been expected to give his life, if necessary, to defend the senator. He'd come very close to doing just that. His Secret Service colleague, Ben Tripoli, had made the ultimate sacrifice, having been literally blown to pieces in the blast.

I'd come to ask him about the bombing, accompanied by Peter Reynolds and a CIA liaison guy, Joe Ibbotson, one of those jittery people who seem never to keep still. Peter looked like a chunky sumo wrestler next to Ibbotson, who was thin to the point of male anorexia. After the shortest of acquaintances, I wanted to slap him. Ibbotson continually shuffled his feet, checked that the knot of his tie was in place, moved his shoulders and stretched his neck. After ten minutes in his company it was all I could do to stop myself from yelling, "Will you stop that!"

"The doctors fully expect to save Foster's eyesight," Ibbotson had said in his high, reedy voice before we entered the hospital room, "but he can say goodbye to an active career." He jiggled around a bit, then added, "He'll get early retirement." Flashing unnaturally white teeth, he'd all but jabbed me in the ribs with his elbow. "Great work if you can get it, uh?"

Now, looking down at the injured man, I doubted Chip Foster would look at it that way. He'd sustained a severe concussion, facial injuries, a fractured sternum, two snapped ribs and lung lacerations. His left ulna had been broken and his right hand shattered. Add to that severe skin burns, and his discomfort, even with heavy duty painkillers, must have been extreme.

"Chip, old pal," Ibbotson said, bouncing around the bed like a demented pogo stick, "Got Agent Cleever and Dr. Reynolds from ASIO here with me. A few questions, that's all. Okey-dokey?"

"Sure. Ask away." Foster's voice was stronger than I expected.

Peter said hello, then nodded to me. "I'm Denise Cleever," I began. "I'm so sorry to meet you under such circumstances."

Foster gave a half smile. "Nice name, Denise. You sound good-looking."

"She's ravishingly beautiful," said Peter, with a wicked grin in my direction.

Ibbotson, absently smoothing his tie, said, "About five-nine, blonde, hazel eyes, good figure." When I glared at him, he put up his hand. "Hey, my pal here can't see. Just filling in the gaps."

I pulled up a chair and sat close to the side of the bed. "I know you've been through this a thousand times, Chip, but would you please go through it again?"

He shifted on his bed, and a grimace of pain tightened his mouth. "We were waiting with Senator O'Neven in a separate room. When we were given the all clear, we entered with the senator. Ben Tripoli went first, checking out the crowd near the podium. I brought up the rear, in case an attack came from behind. We had our people in the room watching for anything out of the ordinary, but they saw nothing."

He paused, then said, "The assessment was this function was low-risk. Everything had gone smoothly to this point. There'd been no threats against Senator O'Neven, either here or back in the States. The man wasn't controversial in any way. He didn't stir up strong feelings."

Peter said, "Any public figure, however innocuous, gets at least one crazy's attention."

"Generic threats only," interposed Ibbotson, rocking heel to toe, then back again. "CIA checked exhaustively. O'Neven only scored the loonies who write or email every mother's son in government, no matter who they are."

"When did you first notice the girl?" I asked Foster.

"She caught my eye before she did anything. It was the expression on her face. She was standing in the front of the crowd, gazing at the senator like he was a pop star. Get what I mean? To her, he was something really special. I remember I wondered for a moment if she and O'Neven had a relationship. But then I thought, heck no, the senator wouldn't get his rocks off with anyone but his wife. He was that type."

"Humph," said Ibbotson.

It was impossible to tell whether he meant approval or disapproval by this. I sent him a interrogatory look, and he obliged by saying, "Senator O'Neven was a good, moral man. Not many of us left."

While I was deciding whether he was joking or serious, Peter Reynolds said, "Don't forget me, Ibbotson. I'm a good, moral man too. Just ask Denise."

They smirked at each other; I rolled my eyes. Returning to the task, I said to the man in the bed, "What happened then?"

"The next thing, I saw her on the steps to the podium and Ben Tripoli attempting to stop her. He wasn't fast enough, and she got around him." He coughed, winced, then went on, "She didn't look a threat. I remember thinking she was just a young girl carried away by the occasion, and wanting to touch someone famous."

Ah, jeez, I thought. This guy was expecting a suicide bomber to look dangerous? Appearing harmless was the whole point. To be successful, you couldn't seem to present a potential threat, or you'd never get close to your intended target.

Almost as though he'd read my thoughts, Foster said, "We were taken by surprise, and that shouldn't have happened. It was my failure, and Tripoli's too. That's why the senator's dead."

"Did she seem dazed, or drugged, or high on something?"

"Like I said, she just seemed normal—maybe a bit star-struck on the senator, but that's all."

"Had you ever seen this young woman before? At other functions where Senator O'Neven appeared, perhaps?"

"No, I would have remembered. She was very attractive." He grunted. "Her whole life ahead of her, and she blows herself up. What a waste."

I looked down at his bandaged face. The waste was greater than Josetta Wilson's life. By one appalling act she'd blotted out of existence herself and two other individuals, and had destroyed both the health and career of this man lying here.

"When she was standing at the front of the crowd," I said, "did you see her communicate with anyone? It could be some sort of gesture, or quick look in another direction, or perhaps she spoke to someone near her."

Chip Foster shook his head fractionally, then suppressed a groan. "Sorry, I've got a hell of a headache."

His voice was appreciably weaker. On the other side of the bed, Joe Ibbotson caught my eye and mouthed, "Cut it short."

I nodded to him, then said to Foster, "You didn't see anyone who could have been an accomplice?"

"No. I wasn't watching her closely, so there could have been someone. I can't help you there."

ASIO had gone through the guest list with a fine tooth comb and turned up no one of any interest, but the Australia-America Friendship Alliance members manning the entrance door had been

20

so slack about checking whether people had valid invitations to the function that anybody looking the part could have got in.

Foster was clearly exhausted, so I asked my final question. "Can you think of anything, however insignificant, that might be of help?"

"She said something as she put her arm around Senator O'Neven's neck. Tripoli might have heard what it was, because he was closer. I only know it was something short. Maybe the video got something."

Unfortunately the back of Josetta Wilson's head was on screen when she spoke. The TV cameras had only shown Senator O'Neven's astonished face the split second before he died. The microphones on the speaker's desk had picked up something faintly, and the audio was still being enhanced.

"Thank you, Chip," I said, getting up from the chair. "If you think of anything—"

"I'll call." He gave a weak chuckle. "Ibbotson says you're a looker. How about a date?"

I patted his uninjured hand. "Just concentrate on getting well."

"Yeah. I'll do that."

I felt a rush of sympathy for Foster. He believed he'd failed his duty. His body would never be the same. I wanted to say to him, "Someone masterminded this atrocity. I'll get them, I promise you."

I didn't speak, just squeezed his fingers and left the room.

Outside, Joe Ibbotson, his lanky form jiggling in place, said to me, "See you again, I hope, Denise." He gave me a sly smile. "You know how important liaison is between our two countries."

"You're wasting your time," said Peter, amused. "How can I put it delicately? Let's just say Denise plays for the other team."

Ibbotson blinked, then light dawned. "Oh, shit," he said. "Say it isn't so."

"It's so." I gave him my best insincere smile. "But heavens, how you tempt me!"

21

CHAPTER THREE

I was staying in Sydney to have a couple of sessions with a voice coach to give my normal Aussie accent a slight American flavor. My undercover personality, Dr. Constance Sommers, though born and educated in Australia, had spent quite some time in the States and Canada as a visiting psychotherapist at various small clinics treating anorexia and similar disorders.

In addition, to make it more likely that Graeme Thorwell would open up to her, Dr. Sommers had apparently worked at the Brindesi Institute in North Carolina, a decidedly shady right-wing organization. It was rumored that the Institute made most of its income through the instruction of foreign nationals in the refinements of psychological torture and extreme techniques of intelligence gathering. The Brindesi Institute was so secretive that there would be no confirmation or otherwise that a Dr. Sommers had ever been on staff.

Of course, there was no Constance Sommers, but a paper trail had been established that proved she not only existed, she was pretty damn good at her job. Dr. Sommers didn't have a medical degree, but a PhD, hence the "doctor." So, although presumably familiar with psychotropic drugs, she would not be called upon to write prescriptions, and if I made some error about medications and their specific uses, I could explain it away.

"Am I to be called Connie?" I asked Cynthia, my control. She'd come up to Sydney to brief me, and was staying in the same rather shabby safe house as I was.

I would have much preferred the comforts of a hotel room with room service, but I'd been informed for security reasons I had to stay here. Privately, I didn't think it was anything to do with keeping me out of the public eye, but was to save money, as lately ASIO's operating budget had been stressed by additional costs of fighting international terrorism.

"You're Connie to intimates," Cynthia said with a grin. "Constance to everyone else."

I looked at her angular body and spiky hair with my usual interest. This was caused, I'd long ago decided, by the lure of the unattainable. Because Cynthia was an unknown quantity, and, in her own odd, idiosyncratic way, extraordinarily attractive, I had a long-term, slow-burning yen for her that almost certainly would never be satisfied.

"Speaking of intimates," I said, "is Constance Sommers straight?"

"The background we've given you hinted bi, just to give you some room to maneuver."

"Whoopy-do," I said, somewhat derisively. "You've doubled my chances of sacrificing my all for my country."

"Let's not go there," said Cynthia.

I felt myself redden slightly. It was my duty to be entirely forthcoming in de-briefings after each of my undercover assignments, however I had to admit there were a few little items I'd deemed too private for ASIO files. Still, Cynthia had a pretty fair idea I'd sometimes mixed pleasure with business when out in the field.

There was, I noted, a mocking smile on her lips. It was clearly time to accomplish a quick change of subject. "Do you think a team of grandmother interior decorators were let loose in here?" I asked, making a wide gesture to indicate the furnishings of the dingy lounge room in which we were sitting.

"I'd reckon *great* grandmothers," Cynthia said, glancing around. "Most of the furniture looks pre-World War II, don't you think?"

It did. Bulbous, heavy lounge chairs and matching sofa were upholstered in a hideous, faded flower design. Pressing in from all sides was heavy, dark furniture of no particular style. A glass-fronted cabinet held dusty china figurines. My favorite, I'd decided, was a shepherdess with crook, whose face showed astonishing stupidity. In IQ she was plainly beaten by the lamb decoratively arranged at her feet.

Cynthia wrenched my attention away from such contemplations by saying, "I imagine you discussed the subject of suicide bombers with Estelle Decker."

"Estelle says Josetta Wilson is an anomaly as far as suicide bombers go. She wasn't a member of a culture where such behavior is actively encouraged. Estelle thinks Josetta was manipulated so she embraced the concept of killing Senator O'Neven as her own idea, her mission in life."

Cynthia didn't look as if the idea the bomber had been deliberately programmed to murder was a new concept. Undoubtedly she'd already discussed all this with Dr. Estelle Decker long before I'd met with the good doctor. Over the years I'd learned Cynthia almost always knew what was going on, although she rarely disclosed how much she knew about any particular subject. She'd been seriously miffed when Peter Reynolds had learned about the Anita Hutching case before she did.

And more than anything, Cynthia hated surprises. Unfortunately, I often delivered them. Sometimes I wondered why she remained my control, and didn't pass me off to someone else in the organization.

"We know this wasn't a solo effort," I went on. "Someone provided her with the device. Someone drove her to the location. And someone was watching to make sure everything went smoothly."

Fragments of the bomb had been painstakingly collected from the scene and from the human bodies blasted by the explosion. It turned out to be quite sophisticated, as bombs go. One fascinating thing had been discovered: the bomb had been rigged to be detonated by a trigger shaped in the form of a loop, but it had a failsafe mechanism—it could also be detonated by a signal sent from a remote control.

The logical conclusion was that an observer had been close enough to see her approach the target and had been ready to set off the bomb if she failed to do it herself. By some bizarre twist, Josetta's detached forefinger had been recovered, still curled through what remained of the loop forming the trigger. The assumption was she had been the one to detonate the device, but even if she'd changed her mind at the last moment, the result would have been the same.

After the senator's assassination, the streets around the building and all local parking structures were sealed. As people returned to their cars, their identities were verified, they were questioned and then allowed to leave. Eventually no vehicle remained—not even a bicycle. This meant Josetta had either walked, used public transport, or been taken to the location in a vehicle.

All the recordings made by private security cameras in the area had been analyzed, frame by frame. Taxi records had been perused. An appeal had been launched through the media to ask anyone who'd been in the vicinity, or at the function itself, and had taken photographs to come forward. The hope was, of course, that someone snapping a casual shot might catch a face in the crowd who would turn out to be someone of interest to Australian or American intelligence agencies. So far none of these measures had come up with anything useful.

Cynthia and I were discussing this when Peter Reynolds strolled in. "You women," he said, shaking his head. "You just loll around while poor fools like me wait on you hand and foot."

"You're providing food?" I heaved myself out of the armchair. "I'm starving."

"It's my idea of a gourmet meal," Peter said. "Pizza and beer. Then cheesecake."

"Oh, God!" Cynthia's shudder wasn't for effect.

Peter patted her shoulder. "Don't you worry, Cyn old girl," he said. "For you there's a lovely chopped salad, to be followed by fresh fruit, all organically grown, of course."

"Are you a vegetarian?" I said, amazed that I'd not realized this before. When I thought about it, Cynthia looked like a vegetarian, though if asked what I meant by that, I wouldn't be able to say.

"Is that a problem for you?" Cynthia asked, her eyes narrowing. It seemed I'd hit a nerve.

"Oh, heavens no," I said with haste. "Some of my best friends, and all that."

"Yes?"

I beamed at her. "You give me something to aspire to, Cynthia," I said. "As you know, I already have purity of mind. Now your example encourages me to aim for purity of body, as well."

She gave me a cool look. "You'd better get used to calling me Zena, Constance." Zena was the contact name she would be using for this assignment.

"You must call me *Connie*," I said. "I count you as one of my intimates, Zena."

"Zena?" said Peter. "Why does that name sound familiar?"

I clapped my hand to my heart. "Warrior princess and smiter of evil ones," I announced.

Peter took my arm. "Low blood sugar," he said to Cynthia. "It's clear she's hallucinating. I'm a trained psychiatrist, so I recognize the symptoms immediately. The sooner we get some pizza into her, the better."

After we'd eaten, Peter sat me down to continue my crash course of what every good psychotherapist should know. Fortunately I'd studied quite a bit of psychology while at university, so it wasn't all foreign to me, and I could toss around names like Freud, Skinner,

Piaget, Pavlov, Jung, Maslow and so on without feeling I'd made a total fool of myself. In a way it was like being a lowly student again, with Peter playing professor and handing me multitudes of photocopied pages for later study.

We skipped through motivations, stress and coping; skimmed the surface of maladaption and abnormal behavior; had a cursory look at the physical-mental-emotional effects of legal and illegal drugs.

We did linger on disorders found in the young. There seemed so many of these—retardation, impaired development, disruptive behavior, excessive anxiety, eating disorders. Young people, like their elders, suffered from irrational panic, phobias, obsessive-compulsive behavior, post-traumatic stress. Kids could be bipolar, they could be clinically depressed, they could be neurotic, paranoid, schizophrenic. Their personalities could be antisocial, histrionic, narcissistic . . ."

"Jeez," I said, "the wonder is that any of us grow up to be even halfway normal."

"Ah-hah!" Peter pointed his finger at me. "What have I told you about that word?"

"It's a socio-cultural construct," I said pedantically. "Behavior and attitudes considered normal in one society, may be considered distressingly abnormal in another."

"So, Denise, are you normal?" Peter asked.

"Not a chance. I work for ASIO, don't I? It follows automatically I must be mad." I gave him a pretend frown. "And my name, I must point out, is Constance. You may call me Connie if you wish, but only when we're alone."

There was an element of gravity in my request. Soon I'd *be* Dr. Constance Sommers. I had to answer to that name as though it were my own, even when tired, distracted, or confused. Name was such an integral part of self—even in a coma a person would react to his or her name. When someone said Connie, or Constance, or Dr. Sommers, I had to respond immediately. Failure to do so would breed suspicion.

Obediently, Peter said, "So, Connie, are you normal?"

"Not a chance. I'm a psychotherapist aren't I? Mad as a hatter."

27

Peter was a great believer in role-playing. He found a spare room, moved furniture around until two ugly brown lounge chairs faced each other about three meters apart, plunked a table with a large box of tissues on it near one, and said to me, "Okay, just imagine you've consulted a therapist because of ongoing emotional problems, and this is your first session."

"Wouldn't it be better if I were playing the therapist?" I inquired. "That's what Dr. Constance would be doing."

"You need to see it from both sides of the couch," said Cynthia, amusing herself with this observation, but not me. I was feeling ridiculously uneasy about this role play.

"As a rule we don't use couches," said Peter. "Face-to-face appears to be much more effective." He frowned at Cynthia, who had established herself in one corner as an observer. "You're not going to comment on things, are you? You'll interrupt the flow."

"My lips are sealed."

Peter sent me into the hallway, said, "Think yourself into the part," and shut the door in my face. A moment later he opened it. "Ms. Sommers, do come in. I'm Dr. Peter Reynolds, but please call me Peter. May I call you Constance?"

Out in the hall, I'd decided to be a sullen, uncooperative patient. "If you like," I said with a shrug.

He ushered me to the chair with the table and open box of tissues. "Please make yourself comfortable."

I eyed the chair. "I'll try, but it'll be difficult."

Peter sat down opposite me, his body language relaxed, his expression open. "Why have you come here today, Constance?"

"Dunno. You tell me."

He smiled, asked me about my family. I replied tersely. Peter raised his eyebrows interrogatively. "You say you have a brother?"

"Yes. Martin."

"And your relationship with Martin, would you call it close?"

I was suddenly aware of Cynthia sitting in the corner, watching, plus the disconcerting fact I was starting to feel a bit upset. Martin and I had never been loving siblings. To begin with, he was much older. That wouldn't have been a problem if I hadn't been too independent for Martin's liking, and far too inclined to ignore his advice—not that this stopped him from offering it. We'd grown increasingly estranged over the years, and now we rarely communicated at all.

"We're not close," I said.

"How does that make you feel, not being close?"

"I don't think about it."

And so it went on, with me grimly parrying questions, and Peter, his equanimity undiminished, inquiring in various ways how I felt about my life until I finally snapped, "Intensely irritated. With you. That's how I feel."

"Can you explain why you feel irritated?"

"Ah, jeez! You're not telling me this sort of routine works, are you?" I hopped up and hurled the tissue box at him. "This role play is over, kaput, finished."

"Excellent!" Peter, who'd caught the box before it hit him, beamed at me. "Now Denise . . . Sorry, *Connie*. If you have a session where a subject terminates proceedings, perhaps by storming out of the room, remain calm and approachable. Let the patient come back to you. This may not be until the next scheduled session, when you, as the therapist, gently introduce what happened last time you met and—"

"Don't tell me. Let me guess. I ask, 'And how did that make you feel?'"

Peter raised his eyebrows to Cynthia. "By George, I believe she's got it."

❧

29

In the next few days I pored over case studies, watched training videos of various staged sessions between psychiatrists and patients, and generally familiarized myself with the procedures and personnel of Easehaven Clinic.

Estelle Decker had given me a copy of her textbook *The Malleable Brain: A Study of Psychological & Physiological Manipulation.* I learned that normal brain functions can be modified by fasting, or consuming an extreme diet, for example, one abnormally high in sugars. Prolonged physical discomfort or pain affected the brain, as did the continuous chanting of mantras, or imposed patterns of breathing such as those taught in advanced yoga. Lighting and sound effects, certain drugs, even incense, had measurable effects.

In a medical setting, psychiatric treatments intended to alter mental function included administering electric shocks to the brain—a technique enjoying contemporary rehabilitation after the horrors depicted in *One Flew Over a Cuckoo's Nest*—or inducing insulin shock by injection.

I was particularly interested in her chapter of hypnotism, as I was to have two training sessions with a hypnotherapist. I had to learn fast. Hypnotherapy had been given as one of Constance Sommers clinical tools.

Dr. Terrance Jeffrey didn't fit my mental picture of a hypnotist. I had in mind a bouncy, super-confident, noisy person with piercing, dark eyes. Perhaps he'd be twirling a waxed mustache and murmuring something like, "Relax, I have you in my power. You will hear only my voice . . ."

Dr. Jeffrey, however, was a smooth, quietly self-assured man. If he had any rough edges they weren't apparent. His manner was affable, easy. His thinning hair was combed back neatly, his features were pleasant, but forgettable. His voice, like his smile, was restrained but sincere.

"Tell me what you know about hypnotism," he said, tenting his fingers and looking at me with an earnest interest that implied there'd be nothing else in the world he'd rather be doing but sitting here with me.

We were in his consulting rooms. Like Jeffrey, there was nothing to excite in the bland décor—no discordant colors, no furnishing surprises.

"I don't know much except what I've read in Estelle Decker's *Malleable Mind*. She says hypnotism isn't unconsciousness, but a form of relaxation that could be described as an altered state of conscious awareness. While in that altered state the person is much more suggestible than usual."

"Very good," said Dr. Jeffrey.

I smiled, feeling rather like a pupil who'd done her homework. "Truthfully, Dr. Jeffrey, the only hypnotism I've seen first hand was a stage hypnotist. He put volunteers into trances and showed how they didn't feel pain, or made them do silly things to amuse the audience. I don't suppose that's anything like what you do."

"The principles behind both performance hypnotism and medical hypnotism are very much the same. Of course a stage hypnotist has the advantage of selection. He uses tests to choose the few who are particularly susceptible subjects. Hypnotherapists have no such luxury. We have to accept all patients who come to us for help."

"So there are people who can't be hypnotized?"

"Almost everybody can, with the exception of the insane. Of course, the depth of the trance may vary. Some people will never go beyond a light or medium stage. A deep trance can be induced in only a small proportion."

He handed me a photocopied article. "This is a recent report condensing the research findings on the efficacy of hypnotherapy in various therapeutic applications. You will see how accepted it has become for the treatment of acute and chronic pain, anxiety, stress related illness, nausea associated with cancer medications, panic disorders, insomnia, phobia, obesity, eating disorders, and so on."

As I glanced at the pages, he went on, "But of course this doesn't address your problem. I gather you are to be impersonating a psychotherapist who has used hypnotism in her practice."

"That's about it, Dr. Jeffrey," I said. "You've got a couple of sessions to transform me." I grinned. "Maybe you should hypnotize me to speed things up."

He smiled his moderate smile. "That's an excellent idea."

That gave me a little jolt. I didn't like the idea of being hypnotized. Not one bit. "Are you sure you can hypnotize me?" I asked.

"I'm confident I can. All intelligent people can attain at least a light trance state. And let me point out this has nothing to do with willpower, strong or weak. Hypnotism works on the imagination, the ability to visualize. The hypnotherapist simply makes suggestions. The imagination acts upon them."

"I've got a hypothetical question, Dr. Jeffrey. What if you put me under, and then—heaven forbid—you keel over with a heart attack? What happens then?"

"Your trance would merely turn into ordinary sleep. After a time you'd wake up, none the worse for wear."

I wasn't happy, but I couldn't think of a reasonable excuse to avoid being a guinea pig. And I had to admit I'd learn a lot more by experiencing hypnotism myself. "Let's get it over with," I said.

In spite of all my doubts, the whole thing turned out to be pretty much a non-event. Dr. Jeffrey chatted to me about various methods of inducing relaxation, then asked me to close my eyes. He had a pleasantly modulated voice, and after a while I began to drift into the nice drowsy state that occurs just before sleep. I didn't doze off, however, but continued to hear Dr. Jeffrey's voice quite clearly.

When he asked me to open my eyes, I said, "It didn't work, did it? I mean, I wasn't really hypnotized."

"How do you feel?"

"Good. Very good, in fact." I had to admit I was more relaxed than I'd been for ages.

"You were in a light trance." Seeing my doubt, he continued, "Let's say, for example, you'd been a patient consulting me about her insomnia. While you were in that light hypnotic state, your mind would be much more receptive to the suggestions I would be making to help you overcome periods of sleeplessness. In your case I suggested you should let go things that were stressing you, and relax."

"So hypnotism is basically giving advice—the difference being it's actually listened to, for once."

He smiled. "You could say that."

"I'm a bit disappointed."

"How so?"

"You never once said, 'Ah hah! I have you in my power.'"

"That's because I didn't."

"So, Dr. Jeffrey, you couldn't make me do something I didn't want to do?"

"I couldn't force you to go against your personal code of ethics," he said reassuringly. "Hypnosis creates extreme cooperation between doctor and patient, however if the doctor were to suggest something the patient would reject when not in a trance, the patient will similarly reject it when hypnotized."

I could see he was painting a rather rosy picture. I said, "But what if the person's waking self *does* believe in something morally wrong, for example, murder as a justifiable political strategy? And then, when hypnotized, the person is told he or she must act on that belief?"

"It depends on many variables."

"Don't hedge, Dr. Jeffrey. What do you really think?"

Frowning, he considered the question, then said, "I'm afraid the person would be likely to comply."

Joe Ibbotson came to see me the day before I left for Easehaven. We sat down in the safe house's ugly lounge room.

"No way do I want to compromise the operation," he said, his fingers tapping a tattoo on the dusty arm of the heavy lounge chair, "but I trained with the agent we sent into Easehaven. She's quite a gal, and I'd sure hate it if anything happened to her."

Cynthia/Zena, who was sitting in on our conversation, frowned. "Joe, may I remind you that the CIA put this agent in place without consulting ASIO. Of course we'll do what we can, but our primary aim is to investigate the possibility that Graeme Thorwell has found a way to produce brainwashed subjects who'll act as human bombs, or use a vehicle as a lethal weapon, killing themselves in the process."

"I know that," Ibbotson said, tapping his feet in time with the rhythm of his fingers. He sent a faint smile in my direction. "Hey, no one would argue that Constance has a lot on her plate. All I'm asking is that Madison Petrie not get lost in the shuffle."

"I'll do what I can," I said.

Ibbotson got to his feet as if some spring mechanism had propelled him out of his chair. Seizing my hand, he said, "I knew I could count on you."

I disentangled my fingers. "What's your best guess at what's happened to her?"

He shifted from foot to foot, his thin face intense. "Let's put it this way—best case scenario, our agent is still collecting intelligence, but can't get it out to us at the moment." His expression became grim. "Worse case, the SOB has killed her."

Zena, obviously keen to get rid of him, cleared her throat. "Joe, I don't like to hurry you, but . . ."

"I'm outta here!" He leaned over to squeeze my shoulder. "You take care, now."

Zena shepherded him toward the door. Before he left the room, Ibbotson turned back to say to me warmly, "I'll be thinking of you, Constance."

After he'd gone, Zena said to me, "You've certainly got a fan in Joe Ibbotson."

"Must be my irresistible personality."

"Must be," said Zena with a grin.

CHAPTER FOUR

Easehaven showed the generous application of much money from its impressive entrance gate to the sprawling, two-story building set among impeccable gardens. There was even a small lake with black swans. I knew from photographs and maps that Easehaven was built on a headland, but there was no view of the ocean from this vantage point.

The guard at the gate had obviously called up to the house. Even before the gravel stopped crunching under my wheels, a diminutive, stocky woman wearing a tailored pink uniform came striding out the front door to greet me.

I'd rented a generic car at Sydney International Airport after going through the charade of collecting my bags from the carousel loaded with luggage from the Qantas flight from Los Angeles. Even though no one from the clinic was supposed to be meeting me there, I had to act as though I was being observed. This was the first rule of undercover work: always assume someone is watching.

It was a Tuesday morning, the traffic hadn't been impossible, so I'd made good time up the Sydney-Newcastle Freeway. About halfway to Newcastle I'd left the freeway and driven toward the coast. I'd stopped for a quick lunch at a McDonald's, so my inner woman would be nourished when I arrived at Easehaven.

"Good trip?" the woman inquired as I got out of the car. She had a round, doll-like face, wide blue eyes, and tightly curled brown-gray hair. Seizing my hand, she shook it hard. "I'm Phoebe," she said, "Phoebe Murdoch. Administrator." She gestured to the building behind her. "Manage the show. Make sure everything runs smoothly."

She spoke with the strangled vowels I associated with the British upper class. I replied with the Aussie-American accent I'd been practicing in the car. "The trip was fine. I'm Constance Sommers, as you must already know. Great to meet you, Ms. Murdoch."

"Oh, *Phoebe*, please. We don't stand on ceremony here at Easehaven." She'd seen me glance at her very pink uniform, as she went on to say, "Studies have shown the color pink has a soothing effect upon the agitated or depressed." She put a hand to her rose-bud mouth with a cry of amusement. "Oh, what am I saying? Of course you must know that, Dr. Sommers!"

"Do call me Constance," I said, vainly trying to recall what I knew— if anything—about color therapy. Shall I take my luggage . . . ?" I indicated the boot of the car.

Phoebe looked almost shocked. "No, of course you're not to worry about your suitcases. Do leave the keys in the ignition. Sean will park your vehicle for you, and take your things to your room. In the meantime, have you had lunch?"

"Yes, I stopped on the way."

"Well, I'm sure you'd enjoy a refreshing cup of tea. Or has your time in America accustomed you to coffee?"

"Tea would be wonderful. Thank you." Reminding myself I was supposed to have recently spent many hours on a trans-Pacific flight, and then driven myself here to the Central Coast, I politely smothered a yawn.

"What can I be thinking? Of course you're exhausted after your long journey." She turned to a pale, pimply young man standing deferentially to one side, his hands clasped in front of him. He seemed to have materialized out of thin air, but I assumed he'd come silently out of the building while my attention had been on Phoebe. "Sean, Dr. Sommers has luggage in the boot of her car. You're to take it up to her room immediately, before you park the vehicle."

"'Kay."

Irritation swept across Phoebe's porcelain face. "How many times have I told you, Sean? How many times? The appropriate reply for you to make in this situation is 'at once' or 'immediately.' The colloquialism 'okay' is completely unacceptable."

"Sorry."

A silence fell. I hid a smile. At last Phoebe said, grimly, "I'm waiting, Sean."

Sean frowned, then his face cleared. "At once. Immediately." He waited to see the effect this had.

"That's much better, Sean. Now, get along with you."

Phoebe waited until he had my bags out of the car and had taken them inside before she said to me, "Always a problem, you understand, getting suitable staff out here so far from the city lights. And as soon as you train them"—she broke off to throw her hands in the air—"they're off to greener pastures. It's a continual worry, as you might understand."

I made an sympathetic, must-be-awful-for-you sound.

Phoebe took my elbow to lead me into Easehaven. "You must tell me all about America. I've traveled the world, but I've never been there."

"So you don't know Dr. Thorwell from the States?"

"Oh, no, my dear. I started at the Paris clinic as an assistant manager, and when this opportunity presented itself, naturally I seized it."

"You didn't like Paris?"

"Paris is one of the great cities of the world. It's the French I can't stand." She bestowed on me a sunny smile. "Do you speak French, Constance?"

"Only a little. School-girl standard, really."

True, French wasn't my favorite foreign language—I was far better at Indonesian and Japanese—but I was considerably more adept than my modest statement would suggest.

Phoebe paused in the entrance way. "But surely, Constance, you did spend some time in Canada. A clinic in Montreal, wasn't it? You would have needed some French there, I'd venture."

I knew that at Graeme Thorwell's behest, Phoebe had checked out the credentials of Dr. Constance Sommers. ASIO's elaborate web of evidence, established with the CIA's assistance, convinced Phoebe that there was a real, living Constance Sommers who was a highly successful therapist with a sterling reputation. And perhaps with something to hide from her time at the Brindesi Institute.

"Phoebe, you astonish me," I said, smiling. "How in the world did you know I'd been in Montreal?"

"You can blame Dr. Thorwell. He insists that I know everything about every patient, every member of staff. He believes it is vital for clear communications and to avoid misunderstandings. It's just an added little responsibility that takes quite a bit of my time, however I understand Dr. Thorwell's thinking on the matter."

I managed not to give a scornful snort. I didn't believe a word of it. Cynthia—or rather, Zena—had had me study the staff structure at the clinic, as well as all that was known about the patients presently at Easehaven. On paper at least, Phoebe Murdoch's duties were entirely concerned with the day-to-day running of the place. She would need to know food and accommodation preferences of mental health professionals working at Easehaven, but the medical files of patients should surely be verboten to her.

We had walked down a short entrance hall, and were now in the reception area. Light streamed through a huge skylight. The floor was a warm, polished wood. The reception desk was a beautiful, sleek piece of furniture. The waiting area held similarly elegant, smoky-gray chairs and low, glass-top tables. There was a profusion of potted ferns and other indoor plants, all growing, it seemed, with intense enthusiasm. However the walls, I noted with a mental shudder, were pale pink. Next to beige, the color I disliked most in the world would have to be pink, particularly the wishy-washy variety.

"More pink," I said.

"Soothing, isn't it?" Phoebe gazed around with a proprietary air. "Every element in this area is designed to calm the troubled soul."

I indicated the reception desk. "There's no one on duty?"

"We have very strict visiting procedures here at Easehaven. Frankly, Constance, as much as possible we discourage relatives and others interrupting the therapy process. Easehaven is, as its name implies, a haven, a refuge, a place where the damaged come to be made whole."

This sounded like a quote from one of the clinic's brochures. "And do the damaged become whole?" I asked.

"Insofar as is possible. And we achieve near miracles. Even so, I don't need to tell you, Constance, that serious organic problems may be assuaged, but not cured." She looked past me, and exclaimed, "Daphne!"

I turned to see a truly delightful woman. Even the pink uniform she wore didn't dim the impression. She had a slim, compact body and moved with the grace of an athlete. In fact, she'd been a world-class sprinter. I'd seen her photograph in ASIO's Easehaven staff briefing file, and wondered at the time if Daphne Webster would appear as attractive in real life. It was a pleasure to realize she looked considerably better.

Phoebe was busy doing introductions. "This is Daphne Webster, head of our wonderful care team. Daphne, meet Dr. Constance Sommers. You'll recall it was mentioned at our last staff meeting that Dr. Sommers would be joining us here at Easehaven."

Daphne and I shook hands. I felt a slight electric tingle. Static electricity perhaps?

"Daphne," said Phoebe, her doll-like features full of entreaty. "A favor? I've promised Constance a cup of tea to revive her after her long trip, but I do need to check that Sean has placed her luggage in the correct room, and that everything else is in order. Would you mind . . . ?"

"Of course." Daphne grinned at me. "Would you rather a stiff drink?"

"Tea will be fine."

As we walked down a wide corridor—pink, naturally—I said, "Do call me Connie."

"Really? Constance sounds so elegant."

"Elegant I ain't," I said, looking at her sideways. She had short, dark hair, well-cut so it looked casually tousled, a strong nose, full lips, and a determined chin. I jerked my mind back to business. "Have you been at Easehaven long?"

"Six months. I confess I was seduced by the pay and conditions."

I raised an eyebrow. "Not by Dr. Thorwell?"

Daphne chuckled. "Graeme is spectacularly good-looking, I'll give you that."

"I've never met him," I said.

"No? You're in for a treat."

Before I could decide if Daphne meant this seriously, or was making an ironic comment, we turned a corner and entered a spacious sitting room. The walls, thank God, were pale blue. Comfortable chairs in a darker shade of blue were arranged around low tables scattered through the room. Images on a flat-screen television flickered, but there was no sound. A kitchen area took up one corner.

"Edward," said Daphne, going over to one of the three people sitting in the room, "this is Dr. Constance Sommers. Look after her, will you, while I make tea."

As she headed for the kitchen, Edward popped to his feet, grinning. He wore the ubiquitous pink uniform, and had straw-colored hair flopping across his forehead, a rangy body and extraordinarily large hands and feet.

40

My hand disappeared into his, as he shook it enthusiastically. "Edward Quoint," he said. "And yes, I've got a very unusual name. No idea where it came from."

"Strange. I would have said Edward was quite a common name."

He gave a bark of laughter. "The Quoint, I mean, as if you didn't know!" He suddenly lunged and punched me lightly on the bicep. "You're a bit of a joker, eh, Constance? Be a change around here. The medical staff's inclined toward self-importance, if you get my drift."

Although I knew his real position on the staff, I said, "You're a doctor here?"

"Nah. Nursing staff. Not that they call us that to the patients— who by the way, aren't patients, they're *guests*. To our guests, I'm a member of the guidance facilitators. The Ease Team."

"Ease Team?" I said.

"A hoot, isn't it?" He dropped his voice. "But they take such things very seriously around here, especially Phoebe. You've met Phoebe?"

"I have." I kept a neutral tone, suitable for a visiting therapist.

Edward paused to give me an approving once-over. "We all heard your impressive achievements at the staff meeting yesterday. No one said you were *this* attractive."

"Oh, belt up, Edward." Daphne had arrived with a tray bearing a blue ceramic teapot, three fine china teacups, and matching milk and sugar bowls. There was also a plate of Danish pastries.

We all sat. Daphne poured the tea, handed me a delicate cup, and said, "You might find this hard to believe, but Edward is terrific with the patients. He's the big brother that many of them never had."

That touched a nerve with me. I was still smarting from the mock therapy session with Peter Reynolds. "What if the big brother caused the problem that put them into Easehaven in the first place? Wouldn't Edward playing this role exacerbate the situation?"

They both considered this deeply for a moment. I was puzzled, until I realized I was the authority. The magic appellation of 'doctor' in front of my name gave everything I said in the quasi-medical sphere extra weight. Presuming I didn't blow everything by saying something irredeemably stupid, I could get to like this clout, I decided.

"Ah, here you are!" Phoebe looked down on the three of us with a pleased smile. This faded as she checked the watch pinned on her quite generous bosom. "Edward? Your shift begins in five minutes."

"On my way, Phoebe. On my way."

Phoebe kept her gaze on him as he left the room. "We encourage a casual attitude," she said to me, "but not in all things. Strict punctuality, for example, is paramount, don't you agree?"

"Absolutely. It provides structure to the day, simultaneously implying dependability, reliability, constancy."

"I couldn't have put it better myself." She seemed almost as impressed with these words as I was.

I repressed a desire to say, "It actually sounds like it means something, doesn't it?" Maintaining a serious expression, I asked when I'd be meeting the head of the clinic.

"There'll be cocktails at seven to welcome you. Dr. Thorwell will be there, and of course you'll meet everyone else who's not on duty. Then dinner at eight-fifteen."

"I can't help noticing," I said, "that you refer to Dr. Thorwell in a formal manner, when everyone else is on first name terms."

The fire of a true believer flashed in her eyes. "Graeme Thorwell is a genius," she said. "Others may call him Graeme—indeed, he asks them to do this—but to me he is Dr. Thorwell. He deserves that respect."

"I can hardly wait to meet him," I said. I meant it.

CHAPTER FIVE

After Phoebe had taken me upstairs to my room and demon-strated how the electronic keycard opened the door, she left me with the comment that the afternoon was mine to do with as I chose. Her suggestion was to unpack, have a nice hot shower, and follow this by a good lie down to prepare myself for the evening. I fully intended to unpack and shower, but lying down was out of the question. I was going to spend the afternoon reconnoitering.

My room was very comfortable, without being over-the-top lux-urious. It was furnished simply, but with discerning taste. Outside, the hallway was entirely beige—walls, ceiling and carpeting—so I'd steeled myself for more of the same in here, but fortunately a muted gray-blue wallpaper was teamed with gray-blue carpet of a deeper shade. I had my own private, all-white bathroom and a small walk-in closet. My bedroom window, complete with cushioned window seat, opened to a wonderful view of gardens running up to the cliff edge.

I could hear waves crashing, but could see only the serene blue of the sea.

Phoebe had had plenty of time to search my luggage, but nothing seemed disturbed. She could be waiting until I unpacked, as a search would be easier then. And even if she did scan my things, she wouldn't find anything incriminating. My clothes were unremarkable, my toiletries were American brands. I had a digital camera and a Palm Pilot set up just as Constance Sommers would have it, with addresses, phone numbers, appointment schedules and so on. A fine pair of Steiner binoculars was accompanied by a field guide on North American birds. At Sydney airport I'd purchased a pocket guide on native Australian birds. A hobby of bird-watching had been chosen to give me, if needed, a convincing reason to be wandering around looking at things.

I noted there was a telephone in my room, complete with instructions on how to dial out. This would not be a secure line, so I'd be using it very carefully, if at all. As soon as convenient, my instructions were to go to the nearest large town and obtain a mobile phone—or *cell* phone, as Constance would call it, since she'd spent so much time in North America.

Showered, changed into comfortably loose jeans and much-washed T-shirt—both purchased in the States, as was most of the clothing I'd brought with me—I slung the binoculars around my neck, shoved the pocket guide to native birds in my hip pocket, and set off to explore the grounds and add detail to the mental map I had of Easehaven. I'd studied local maps, architectural drawings, floor plans and aerial photographs. Information on the running of the place had been covertly gleaned from former employees and trades people. Now it was time to translate abstract information into reality.

The gardens were delightful and obviously carefully planned. In the front of the building, sheltered from the ocean breezes, the less hardy flowers and shrubs were planted. When I came around the side of Easehaven and began to walk toward the water, the gardens contained native vegetation accustomed to harsher conditions.

Reaching the edge of the cliff, I looked down to the tumbled rocks below. It was a fall of about twenty meters. As Constance had become familiar with American measurements, I automatically converted the meters into sixty-five feet. Quite high enough to be fatal. Although the day was calm, and only a gentle wind gusted against my face, the sea was up, probably from a storm far out to sea.

With hypnotic regularity, the water, forming white top waves as it neared the land, smashed into the unyielding rock. Not so unyielding, however—unimaginable time and persistence had beaten against the cliff face until the sandstone had collapsed into the waiting water. Judging from the huge boulders below me, this had happened many times.

I turned my back to the restless sea to look back at Easehaven. The building was made up of three wings radiating from a central reception area. There were extensive areas of glass, so I imagined there must be a team of cleaners constantly employed. The wing housing the patients had a lock-down facility to secure seriously disturbed individuals who might hurt themselves or others, but most patients enjoyed private rooms that from architectural plans I'd seen would seem to mirror my bedroom with its walk-in closet and en suite bathroom.

I wondered in which room the CIA's Madison Petrie was confined. As soon as possible I'd have a look at the patient records to see if I could locate her. What I'd do then was problematic. My primary task was directed toward brainwashing activities at Easehaven, not the rescue of another undercover agent.

All Easehaven's patients were accommodated on the premises, but a few members of staff lived off the site. The majority, however, took advantage of the excellent quarters provided by the clinic.

Using my binoculars, I studied the nearest wing until I picked out the window of my room. It was in the center, not the position I would have picked if I'd had the choice. I would have preferred to be adjacent to a stairway, so that I could come and go with less chance of being seen.

The third wing, the furthest from my present vantage point, held counseling rooms, recreation areas, sitting rooms, and kitchen and dining areas. I knew the doctors and nurses ate with the patients, but the rest of the staff had their own, smaller dining room.

A movement caught my eye. Someone had come around the corner of the building and was striding purposefully toward me. I casually swung around to face the sea, putting the binoculars to my eyes. Fortuitously, a sea eagle chose just that moment to ride an updraft. I held it in my field of vision as it rose, wings outspread. What a magnificent creature! For a moment I forgot I was putting on a bird-watching act. White, with gray back and wings, its sleek head and hooked beak outlined against the pale blue sky, it rode the wind.

"Beautiful, isn't it?" said a resonant American voice. I lowered the binoculars. "Dr. Thorwell, I presume," I said, putting out my hand.

He shook it firmly. "It's a pleasure to meet you, Dr. Sommers. Phoebe thought you might have come out this way. I hope you don't mind company."

He'd put on a little weight since the "after" photos Peter had shown me, but the package of chiseled features, thick, dark hair, and incandescent smile, made him amazingly handsome. Even though I knew much of the effect had been achieved by the skills of plastic surgeons, a cosmetic dentist and whoever it was responsible for drilling some sense of style into him, he was still a knockout.

He was wearing dark glasses, but I knew his eyes would be deep cornflower blue, unless he'd neglected to put in his colored contact lenses, in which case they'd be an undistinguished brown.

"Of course I don't mind company," I said. "I've been indulging in a little bird-watching."

"Is this an interest of yours?"

"I'm a rank amateur, frankly. I did quite a bit in North America, but I must say Australian birds are much more familiar to me." I indicated the sea eagle, which was now just a speck high above us. "White-bellied Sea Eagle."

"I'm impressed."

I gave a lighthearted giggle. "Don't be. I grew up on the coast at Bateman's Bay." That, of course, was where my curriculum vitae had Constance Sommers spending her youth.

Pulling the field guide from my hip pocket, I went on, "I'd better check. I'm quite capable of labeling the poor bird something it's not."

Thorwell came to stand beside me so he could look over my shoulder. He was half a head taller than I, and well-muscled. I had a sudden vivid picture of myself pitching over the cliff. It would just take a quick shove, and I'd be fish bait.

"Here it is," I said. "*Haliaeetus leucogaster*, better known as the White-bellied Sea Eagle."

"Let's stroll to the end of the headland," Thorwell said, putting a hand under my elbow.

I casually moved my arm away. What was it around here about touching people? Phoebe had grabbed my elbow too, while steering me into the building when I'd arrived. And she'd done the same thing when showing me the way to my room.

Deprived of my arm, Thorwell shoved his hands into the pockets of his exceedingly well-cut trousers, which he'd teamed with a loose-weave sports shirt and soft leather slip-on shoes—Italian, I guessed. "It's a lovely day for a walk," he said.

I mentally switched myself to light-conversational mode as we commenced our stroll. Prepared though I was to spout professional jargon, this was clearly not the time to do so. "It is beautiful," I agreed. "You're so lucky to have your clinic situated in such a glorious spot."

"It's all because of Fenella van Berg." He glanced over at me with a boyish smile. "She's made this all possible. I can never repay her."

"I believe her daughter's a patient at Easehaven." I could be expected to know this, as my introduction to the clinic had ostensibly been through Fenella van Berg's good offices.

"Rosemary is a guest, Constance, *guest*. I strongly believe the connotations of the word 'patient' create an unfortunate impression of inequality between the medical professional and the subject." He threw me a blinding smile. "May I call you Constance, by the way?"

"Please."

"And I'm Graeme." We strolled a little further before he said, "Rosemary *is* a guest here at the moment. I was wondering if you'd care to sit in on a session I'm having with her tomorrow morning. I would very much value your thoughts on her treatment."

"I'd be delighted."

We reached the end of the headland, and stood to admire the view. The differing blues of sea and sky met in a lovely line. The coastline stretched on either side of us with little beaches and promontories, fading into the distance. It truly was a glorious spot. I could believe such beauty might have a healing effect upon troubled minds, and said so to Graeme Thorwell.

"Indeed. Easehaven has been worth all the mountains of red tape we had to go through before we were permitted to build on this site." He chuckled, adding, "And there's no denying money can grease the wheels."

"The more money, the better the lubrication, I imagine," I said.

This earned an appreciative laugh. "A woman of the world, I see."

The peace was jarred by a ringing sound. Thorwell snatched a phone out of his pocket and flipped it open. "Yes?" He listened, his expression changing from mild irritation at the interruption to something approaching concern. "When? Yes, of course. Make all the necessary arrangements."

Returning the phone to his pocket, he said to me, "Fenella will be here at the end of the week. A surprise visit. Rosemary will be pleased."

I'd been assured Fenella van Berg had a firm schedule of obligations in the States that would keep her away from Australia for at least a couple of months. The information she was coming to Easehaven within a few days was therefore quite a jolt.

As Fenella's name had been used to get me into Easehaven, Thorwell would assume I knew her well. And, of course, I'd never set eyes on the woman. I said, "I'd so like to meet her. She's been so kind, recommending me for a position here at Easehaven."

He stared at me, plainly astonished. "You don't know Fenella? But I assumed . . ."

"It was her assistant, Kym Browne, who brought me to Ms. van Berg's attention."

"Her assistant? Yes, I know Kym." He was frowning at me. "Why would Kym recommend you?"

I slid into my story, prepared for just this exigency. "I don't know if you're aware of this, but Kym's a single mother. Over the years, her only son, Paul, has attempted suicide several times. I'd had some excellent successes in that area, and several grateful parents mentioned my name in a support group Kym attended. Paul was under my care for some time, and I'm delighted to say he's now at college, and coping extremely well."

I shut up at this point, knowing I had a tendency to get carried away and embellish stories. This was a dangerous weakness. Over-elaborate explanations were inherently suspicious.

Thorwell seemed both puzzled and put out. "I know Kym, of course, but I had no idea about her son. I would have thought she'd have asked *me* for assistance."

I spread my hands. "She didn't want her employer to know. It's not rational, perhaps, but that's the way she felt at the time. Now, of course, Ms. van Berg is aware of the whole story."

The beauty of the yarn I'd just spun was that it was largely true. Kym Browne did have a son who had been suicidal. Desperate after his last attempt to kill himself, she did take the advice of members of a support group and have her son admitted to an expensive private clinic, where he was successfully treated, although not by Constance Sommers, who didn't exist.

When my cover story was being set up, intensive research of Fenella van Berg and everyone around her had turned up Kym

Browne's heartbreaking problems with her son. Strings had been pulled, and the doctor who had treated Paul had contacted Kym Browne and asked for her assistance in recommending a valued colleague who was relocating to Australia. Kym Browne was told that Dr. Constance Sommers had developed the treatment protocol that had been instrumental in saving her son's life. Would Kym be willing to ask Fenella van Berg to recommend Dr. Sommers for a position at Easehaven Clinic in New South Wales? It had taken little persuasion. Kym had been delighted to accede to this request.

Thorwell's handsome face was still set in a frown. "But Fenella did okay the recommendation?" he asked.

"Of course." I matched his frown with one of my own. "Is there a problem? You must have checked all my credentials . . ."

I knew I'd been thoroughly vetted. Phoebe Murdoch had checked me out meticulously, and the system ASIO had put in place had answered everything satisfactorily.

"No problem," Thorwell said. "I'm a little surprised, that's all. I was led to believe that Fenella knew you personally."

"I'm so sorry. I had no idea you thought Ms. van Berg and I had met." Putting on an expression of embarrassed candor, I said, "If I'd realized this was the case, of course I'd have made it clear immediately that the recommendation came through her assistant." I made a helpless gesture. "If you want me to leave . . ." I didn't actually sob, but I was sure my expression would convince him I was very upset.

It was infuriating when playing a vulnerable little woman worked like a charm. Graeme Thorwell rushed to reassure me. "Not at all! This is merely a simple misunderstanding. I'll clear it up with Fenella when she arrives on Friday."

"Perhaps Kym Browne will accompany her? Kym can confirm everything I've told you."

I could say this without fear my cover would be blown, as I knew Kym Browne would not be coming. Fenella van Berg's assistant had recently received a wonderful job offer she couldn't refuse—a position giving her more money, more autonomy, more status. No matter that this had been manipulated through the American intelligence agencies—it was a genuine offer and Kym Browne had been well advised to take it.

"I don't know if Kym will be with Fenella, but it doesn't really matter. Your qualifications are more than impressive, Constance." He put a warm hand over mine. "Forgive me for being so surprised. It's obviously a misapprehension on my part."

I resisted snatching my hand away. This might be the best-looking guy I'd seen for some time, but underneath the veneer, he was creepy.

He smiled at me; I smiled at him.

Jeez!

CHAPTER SIX

I chose a neat, unassuming outfit for the evening—a simple dark blue dress, moderate heels and minimum jewelry. I knew the location of the dining room from the plans I'd studied, but had no idea where the cocktail hour would be held, so I left my room a little early to look around.

I was pleased to almost immediately encounter Daphne Webster coming out a room three doors down from mine. She was looking quite sensational in black pants and a scarlet top. It seemed I didn't quite disguise my appreciative reaction, as she grinned at me, and said, "You're looking pretty good yourself."

"I beg your pardon?"

Daphne laughed. "Don't act so innocent, Connie. Your reputation's preceded you."

"And what reputation would that be?"

"I'm afraid you'll find our Phoebe's a total gossip. When she was emailing, calling and otherwise making sure you were the skilled therapist you said you were, she managed to slip in a few leading questions. There's always someone willing to dish the dirt."

"No doubt Phoebe jumped to unwarranted conclusions," I said primly. "There *is* no dirt to dish about me. I've led an almost entirely blameless life."

Daphne was eyeing me with a speculative smile. "Oh, yes?"

"I suppose I'd better hear the bad news. Just what was said?"

"Let me just put it this way," said Daphne, "I believe you and I have a lot in common."

I didn't think I was imagining the invitation in her smile. Before I could decide whether or not to play it safe and remain oblivious to any thinly veiled meaning, Phoebe Murdoch appeared at the top of the stairs and advanced toward us. Her stout form was poured into a lacey, coffee-colored dress that displayed quite considerable cleavage.

"Constance!" she exclaimed. "I was just coming to collect you. I realized you'd have no idea where to go for our cocktail hour. It's held in Dr. Thorwell's private sitting room." She cast an approving look at Daphne. "But obviously I need not have worried. I see you're in good hands."

"The best," said Daphne, crinkling her eyes at me.

A mental cautionary bell sounded. I had had lovers in my past—and there was one delightful woman I hoped would be in my future. But this was work, or so I told myself. Then again, Zena would not be at all pleased if I compromised the mission by getting involved with the head of the Easehaven nursing staff. Of course, if there were to be an intelligence-gathering reason to justify such a liaison . . .

"Come along," said Phoebe with a touch of impatience. "Everyone will be keen to meet our new member of staff."

Daphne and I traipsed obediently after her. I checked my mental image of Easehaven's floor plans. Dr. Thorwell's quarters appeared to be considerably more luxurious than anyone else on the staff enjoyed, but I reckoned that was fair. The large entertainment area, where I presumed the cocktail party was being held, had bathroom facilities separate from the rest of the apartment. This was irritating, as I would have loved an opportunity to sneak a look around while supposedly taking a comfort break. There was a smaller sitting room with a basic kitchen attached, a study, a large bathroom with a sunken bath, and lastly, a bedroom with French doors opening onto a private garden.

While I'd been mentally reviewing the floor plans, we'd come down the stairs, turned right, and halted at a beige door bearing the word PRIVATE. Phoebe knocked, saying over her shoulder to me, "For security reasons this door is always kept locked."

Graeme Thorwell himself opened the door. His contact lenses made his eyes very blue. He smiled, showing his excellent dental work. "Come in, ladies! You're the very first to arrive."

Looking gratified, as if she thought he were congratulating her personally for our early appearance, Phoebe said, "This is Dr. Constance Sommers, Dr. Thorwell."

"We've met." We spoke simultaneously.

Phoebe looked from Thorwell to me, clearly disgruntled. "I wasn't told."

I saw Daphne hide a smile.

Thorwell said mildly, "I spied Constance out bird-watching, and thought I'd introduce myself."

"I see."

Phoebe was rapidly proving herself a pint-size tyrant. I waited to see if Graeme Thorwell would slap her down, but his handsome features remained placid.

His administrator's attention had been taken by something other than our failure to inform her of our meeting. Frowning, she said, "Sean hasn't brought the hors d'ouevres from the kitchen?"

"Not yet."

Exasperated, Phoebe mumbled something clearly uncomplimentary about Sean, and turned on her heel. "I'll be back in a moment."

Ignoring Daphne, Thorwell smiled at me. "Do make yourself comfortable, Constance. I'll get you a drink. A glass of wine, perhaps?"

"Dry white, please."

Daphne said wryly, "Looks like I'll have to help myself," and followed Thorwell across the room.

I looked around. The room was luxuriously appointed. A full bar with a black marble top took up most of one wall. Thick, cream carpet cushioned the feet, pale plush chairs and couches invited me to sit and relax. There were low black marble tables scattered around, and, drawing attention immediately, a sculpture that looked to me like a copy of one of Brancusi's stylized birds. Admiring its sleek lines, I decided maybe it *was* a Brancusi. Why not have the genuine article, when one's patron had more money than she could spend in a hundred years?

Phoebe, mouth set in a hard line, reappeared with Sean, whose acne was less noticeable because of his flushed cheeks. Evidently Phoebe had not held back her feelings about his tardiness. Nearly staggering under the weight of a stack of trays, no doubt containing the missing hors d'ouevres, Sean made it to the bar, where he put his burden down with an audible thump.

Phoebe glared. "Sean! Please don't be so careless."

"Sorry."

"Now, we'll be needing extra ice."

"At once," he said. "Immediately."

I thought Phoebe should be pleased Sean had taken to heart her stern admonitions earlier about his appropriate verbal response to a command, but she didn't look at all impressed. To make up for this, I beamed at him. "Well done, Sean."

He gave me a puzzled look, then hurried off. I turned to Phoebe. "Positive reinforcement," I announced. "Reward the desired behavior, thus increasing the likelihood it will be repeated." This was Psych 101, and Phoebe barely repressed the sneer my comment probably deserved.

She gestured imperiously to a girl in a black dress, who apparently had been pressed into service to pass around the food, watched her with a basilisk stare until the young woman sprang into action, then turned to me. "Now that everyone's arriving, allow me to make the introductions."

In just the last few minutes the room had filled with people. Most seemed interested in eyeballing me, so I flashed a general friendly smile as Phoebe steered me toward the nearest group.

Part of my preparation for this undercover assignment had been to study staff photographs and histories, but naturally as I met each person I dutifully repeated his or her name as though attempting to fix it in my mind. I didn't come across Dr. Norah Bradley, and wondered where she might be. Dr. Bradley had been the psychiatrist treating Anita Hutching, the young woman who'd deliberately crashed her vehicle head-on into the car carrying two witnesses about to testify in a multimillion-dollar business scandal.

Apart from Daphne Webster, there were only three of the nursing staff present. The others, I presumed, were on duty or had given the cocktail hour a miss. I'd already met Edward Quoint, who raised his glass to me in a salute. The two others were Isabella Nelson—a lumpy woman with red-brown frizzy hair and a square, homely face, but possessing a beautiful, melodious voice—and Gretchen Hamilton, a hyperactive young woman with extremely low body fat, whose excellent teeth were displayed in an apparently perpetual smile.

Five minutes with Gretchen persuaded me she was one of those exhausting people who is permanently upbeat, no matter what the circumstances. A veritable Pollyanna for the twenty-first century, she had a high, piping voice that rose in pitch the more fervent she became. "I'd just *love* to live in the States! Although it's wonderful here, too, of course! I'm just so totally lucky to be working at Easehaven!"

Mercifully, I was plucked away from this conversation to be introduced to one of Easehaven's psychiatrists, Dr. Lynda Lane.

Lynda Lane actually fitt my idea of how an idealized psychiatrist should look. She was in her late sixties, had a halo of tightly curled white hair, warm brown eyes, and a long, heavily wrinkled face with a wide, thin-lipped mouth. She rather resembled a solicitous hound. She was a noted authority on altered states of consciousness, particularly those brought about by various meditation techniques.

"Well, my dear, what do you think of us all?" she inquired.

"Everyone's very friendly," I said inanely.

"Not everyone." She indicated with a tilt of her head a slight man with stooped shoulders, standing alone. His glance was constantly flickering around the room as though scanning for any potential danger. He had lank, black hair streaked with gray, and translucent skin. I guessed he'd probably shaved for the function, but already his beard showed as a dark shadow.

"Nonsense, Lynda," said Phoebe bracingly. "It's merely that Harry isn't a social animal."

Lynda Lane pursed her lips. "A total inability to empathize is not desirable in a psychiatrist, Phoebe."

Animosity between Lynda Lane and Harry Gerlich hadn't been mentioned in any of the reports I'd read. "Inability to empathize?" I repeated, eyebrows raised.

"It's quite simple," said Lynda. "Harry Gerlich dislikes humankind in general, and individuals in particular."

"Oh, Lynda, no! That's far too exaggerated a view." Although Phoebe wasn't showing quite the respect I would have thought appropriate for a senior member of the medical staff, Lynda Lane didn't seem to notice.

"Dr. Gerlich's shy, perhaps?" I volunteered.

Lynda Lane all but snorted. "Shy? Not the word I'd use."

To forestall further discussion, Phoebe said, "Come and meet Dr. Gerlich, Constance. You can judge for yourself."

Intelligence sources had reported that Harry Gerlich had been involved in questionable activities in South America—Chile and Peru to be exact. There'd been no firm proof, but evidence suggested he had shredded his Hippocratic oath by his whole-hearted participation in a series of experiments carried out on political prisoners. Gerlich's specialty had been research of the effect on human behavior of extra-low frequency waves, or ELFs. Also called infra-sound, these waves are inaudible to humans. They can pass through any barrier, including metal, with ease.

Within a few seconds a subject bombarded by a certain ELF frequency will experience feelings of euphoria. A slight adjustment of the frequency, and this can turn to deep depression. A slightly higher ELF wavelength can induce extreme agitation and violent behavior. Mood and even bodily functions could therefore be controlled by something entirely undetectable to the victims.

Dr. Gerlich watched our approach with a remote expression. To my chagrin, he didn't seem the slightest interested in me, even though I favored him with a radiant smile. When Phoebe announced I was the new member of staff, Gerlich ducked his head, murmured something that could have been "Hello," followed by "Excuse me," and left us to make a beeline for the bar.

Phoebe clicked her tongue. "Sometimes Harry can be a little thoughtless." Suddenly seeming to realize this might appear as if she were joining Lynda in criticizing Gerlich, she added hastily, "Harry's a truly gifted doctor, but perhaps not entirely comfortable in these social occasions."

I glanced over at the bar, thinking how comfortable he looked knocking back what looked like a triple Scotch on the rocks.

The remainder of the hour allotted for the cocktail party passed quickly. Soon the contents of the trays had been exhausted. The noise level intensified. I'd had a couple of glasses of wine—usually my maximum intake of alcohol. I'd noticed that Graeme Thorwell had been tossing the drinks down, so I was on my guard when he made his way over to where Daphne and I were chatting.

"The two most beautiful women in the room," he said with tipsy gallantry, toasting us with his glass. Patting my shoulder with his free hand, he added, "So glad you're joining Easehaven's family, Constance."

"Thank you."

He sent a drunken smile in Daphne's direction. "And we couldn't do without Daphne's contribution."

"You're too kind, Graeme."

He seemed to miss her dry tone, as he said sincerely, "Not at all, Daphne, not at all."

I said cheerfully, "I suppose there'll be a similar function to this as a welcome for Ms. van Berg when she arrives on Friday."

My comment wiped the smile off his face. "An official welcome? I'm not sure Fenella would want that."

"Fenella never has before," said Daphne, obviously enjoying his discomfort. "Last time she visited, I don't believe anyone on the staff saw her—except, of course, for selected personnel."

Thorwell's cheerful mood had entirely disappeared. He lowered his handsome head, looking forlorn. I felt a stab of sympathy until I reminded myself his mood was probably influenced by the level of alcohol in his blood.

Fortunately at that point someone called to him from across the room. Watching him walk away with the exaggerated care of someone quite drunk, I said to Daphne, "Does he have a problem with alcohol?"

She shook her head. "It's rare to have Graeme drink this much. He's anxious about Fenella van Berg coming here on Friday."

"Why? Because her daughter's here?"

"Because Fenella's a capricious bitch."

"Heavens," I said, "that's what I call direct."

She gave me a lazy smile. "You've no idea how direct I can be."

I gave her a polite smile in return. This woman was coming on way too fast. I reviewed what I knew of Daphne Webster. She'd been a schoolgirl sensation in athletics, eventually representing Australia as a hurdler. Married in her late teens to her running coach, divorced three years later. No children. She'd retired from athletics after a serious knee injury, and started a new career in nursing. She had impeccable qualifications and an admirable work history. She'd collected glowing testimonials as to her skills and administrative abilities everywhere she'd been employed. No record of drug-taking or wild behavior. No mention, actually, of anything much in her personal life. Daphne Webster appeared to be entirely dedicated to her profession.

"Please! Everyone to the dining room immediately." Phoebe's clipped English tones cut through the buzz of conversation. It was a welcome message.

"I'm starving," I said to Daphne. Before she could say anything to match the sly smile on her lips, I added, "For food."

It did cross my mind during the rest of the evening—not notable for anything except the excellence of the cuisine and the fact that Graeme Thorwell retired from the scene after the main course—that perhaps Daphne might call by my room later. I ran through various tactics to cope with this eventuality, but my efforts were wasted. There was an emergency with one of Easehaven's more disturbed guests, and Dr. Lynda Lane and Daphne were called away to deal with the problem.

I went to my bed and slept undisturbed. Waking sometime in the middle of the night, I amused myself by being unable to decide whether I should be relieved or disappointed to be left alone this way.

Relief won by a whisker.

CHAPTER SEVEN

The Easehaven accommodations for the patients—or, rather, guests—obviously attained a standard far above that of the medical staff. The sitting room Dr. Thorwell and I had entered was cream and rose, with furniture that was clearly antique. The Impressionist painting over the marble fireplace looked to be the genuine article. A Persian carpet with a beautiful, intricate design lay on a richly polished floor. French windows opened onto a balcony with wrought iron table and chairs. The view of ocean and headlands was breathtaking.

The sole occupant of the room leapt to her feet when we entered. The photographs I'd seen of Fenella's daughter, Rosemary, had not once shown her smiling. In most she scowled. In a few her rather plain face was peevish or bored. This morning, however, Rosemary Lloyd was beaming. Not at me—at Graeme Thorwell.

The adoration in her eyes was almost embarrassing. "Oh, Graeme," she breathed. "I've been waiting to tell you about the dream I had last night."

"Perhaps later. Rosemary, this is Dr. Constance Sommers."

"Hi." She barely spared me a glance. "Graeme, Mom called me." She looked for a moment disconsolate. "She says she'll be here on Friday."

"And how do you feel about that, Rosemary?"

"Oh, you know . . . Mom can be . . ." She lifted her shoulders.

"Your mother can be . . . ?"

"I don't know . . . overpowering. She takes so much of your time and your attention, Graeme." This last sentence was said with a petulant frown.

Ah, hah! my newly created therapist self said to me. *Note how Rosemary is jealous of her mother's influence over Thorwell.*

This wasn't much of an insight, but I felt proud to be making it at all, under the circumstances. This morning I'd awoken with apprehension—no, to be honest, sharp fear. For the first time in my undercover career I found myself seriously questioning if I could play the role expected of me. Hey, a crash course in how to perform as a therapist didn't make me equal to the challenge. Put me in a clinical situation, and I'd probably make a total mess of things.

After breakfast I'd gone to the administration office to become best friends with Teena, who was responsible for medical and staff records. Confined to a wheelchair, Teena was a middle-aged woman with a sweetly resigned face. "Polio," she confided to me. "Thought I'd conquered the devil when I was a kid, but it's come roaring back."

I'd chatted with her for a while, then asked if she'd go to my staff file to check my qualifications had been correctly entered. When she opened the top drawer of her desk before opening the file, I knew that Teena, like so many people, had passwords written down and kept handy, a practice that made security almost non-existent. As she also allowed me to look over her shoulder while she typed in the password, I memorized her finger strokes. At least it was a combination of numbers and letters, and not a name, which was much easier to guess.

I scanned the information she brought up on the screen, agreed that my entirely fictional qualifications were correct, and thanked her. There was a monitor and keyboard for medical staff use, and Teena showed me how to access medical files on the computer. For these I had my own password, as I was a doctor, after all.

I was there ostensibly to look up Rosemary Lloyd, as I'd be seeing her later in the morning, but my real task was to locate Madison Petrie, the CIA plant whose contact with the CIA in the outer world had been broken. I saw she was being held in the maximum security section because of acute psychotic episodes. She was under the primary care of Dr. Thorwell, assisted by Dr. Gerlich.

I made a quick search for Josetta Wilson's name, but any mention of her had been removed from the files. This led me to another person of interest. Since I'd arrived at Easehaven I'd not heard one mention of Dr. Norah Bradley. Was she still at Easehaven? Had something happened to her?

Teena had been fully engaged with the fax, and I was just about to surreptitiously access staff records when Graeme Thorwell had appeared, looking thoroughly hung over. Like me, he wore a white doctor's coat, though his was of a more dazzling white than mine, and better tailored. That morning I'd discovered with relief that pink was not mandatory for doctors.

"Good morning, Dr. Thorwell."

"*Graeme*, please, Constance." He'd managed a faint nod in Teena's direction, then took me aside to say he thought it an excellent idea for me to have a preliminary chat with Rosemary Lloyd without him. "She doesn't relate well to women," he'd said to me. "I think you'll agree after you speak with her that Rosemary's relationship with her mother is the key to this problem."

"Then why would Rosemary be likely to open up to me?"

Hung over or not, his smile was electric. "I'm already convinced you have exceptional skills, Constance. I feel sure Rosemary is more likely to relate to you than any other female here at Easehaven."

Now, twenty minutes later, he was flashing the same electric smile at Fenella's daughter. "Rosemary, I'd like you to have a little private chat with Dr. Sommers. She and I have been discussing hypnotherapy as part of your future treatment protocol. Dr. Sommers is an expert in this area."

I blinked. Thorwell and I had discussed nothing of the sort. What's more, Rosemary didn't strike me as a promising subject for my first attempt at hypnotism.

Rosemary was not happy. "But Graeme, where will you be?"

"Your mother's unexpected visit means there are a few things I have to attend to. I'll return shortly."

"But—"

"Please, Rosemary." His expression was gently pleading. "For me?"

Pouting, she said reluctantly. "All right. But I expect you back here soon."

When the door closed behind him, she turned to me with a resentful look. "What's your name, again?"

"Constance Sommers. I'd like it if you called me Constance."

Rosemary flung herself down on a graceful little sofa that seemed too dainty to take the weight of her solid body. "If you like." She turned her attention to the sofa, and began to pick at the upholstery fabric.

Jeez, this was promising. She was in full sulk mode, like a thwarted child. Well, at least I knew one subject guaranteed to be of interest. Sitting down at a chair opposite her, I said, "You've known Graeme a long time, haven't you?"

"Uh-huh."

"And you introduced your mother to Dr. Thorwell. Is that right?"

Rosemary didn't deign to look at me. She snapped, "Why are you wasting your time asking me this, if you know it already?"

Dr. Jeffrey's words came back to me. "Always remember a hypnotherapist must have confidence. Any doubt will be sensed by the patient. Remain pleasant and unruffled, no matter what your patient says or does."

Even Dr. Jeffrey would be challenged by this one. However, taking his advice to heart, I refused to be daunted by Rosemary's truculent demeanor, saying cheerfully, "Over the years I've heard so much about Dr. Thorwell's brilliant work. Frankly, I feel quite honored to be able to join his team here at Easehaven."

Apparently I'd hit the right laudatory note. Rosemary actually looked up. "Anyone would be lucky to work with him. Graeme is a wonderful doctor." She took a deep breath. "He's a wonderful man."

I had the stray thought that maybe Graeme Thorwell was being groomed by Fenella to marry this lumpish, discontented woman. It was clear Rosemary would have no objections to this union. I imagined Thorwell, however, might have quite a few.

I leaned forward, saying in a confiding tone, "Dr. Thorwell was telling me earlier he's known you for many years."

He hadn't said any such thing, of course, but I knew it to be true. With an empathetic smile, I went on, "How very interesting it must be for you to have seen such major changes in his life."

"My mother's money, you mean?"

Well, that was right to the point. I said smoothly, "It's true her generosity has made so much possible." I gestured at the room. "Easehaven Clinic, for example."

"There are two other clinics, you know." A small, proud smile lightened her stolid expression. "Graeme's in charge of all of three."

"Have you visited them all?"

Rosemary shrugged. Apparently the clinics were not of major interest to her. I switched back to the sure thing. "Dr. Thorwell seems to have everything," I said with admiration. "A rewarding career in medicine, financial security, good looks . . ."

"Mom gave Graeme a total makeover." With a tinge of hostility, she added, "She likes to do things like that—turn people's lives upside down."

"A makeover?"

My girls-together-gossiping routine was bearing fruit. Rosemary nodded solemnly. "I knew him before the plastic surgery and personal trainer."

I looked appropriately surprised. "Dr. Thorwell's had plastic surgery? Really?"

"It's true. When I first met him, he didn't look like he does now." She hastened to add, "Oh, he was very nice before—just not quite as handsome."

That was stretching things. I'd seen the photographic evidence, and Graeme Thorwell had not been physically prepossessing prior to surgery.

"My mom made Graeme do it. He doesn't really care about looks, you know."

This was said with such an earnest tone I felt a twinge of compassion. Surely Rosemary wondered why her mother hadn't lavished such attention on her own daughter. If anyone would benefit from a makeover, Rosemary would.

"He might not care," I said, "but he *is* awfully handsome."

I'd gone too far. Rosemary's face darkened as she reassessed my status in her world. I'd started off as Constance Sommers, therapist, morphed into Constance, confidant. Now I was Constance Sommers, rival.

"You think so?" She heaved herself to her feet and began to pace with heavy steps about the room. "So you've known Graeme—how long?"

With a sunny, unconcerned smile, I said, "We met for the first time yesterday."

Rosemary halted. "Yesterday?"

"On the headland, actually. I was admiring the view."

She brushed this bit of human interest aside. "So you don't really know Graeme at all, do you?"

"Only for his professional achievements."

She continued to glower at me. I managed a girlish laugh. "Between you and me," I said, "he'd tempt me a little, if I wasn't irredeemably gay."

"Gay? You?" Rosemary cocked her head, regarding me with a deeply suspicious expression. "You're too good-looking to be a lesbian."

Oh, please! Clearly here was a narrow-minded woman who embraced stereotypes ardently. She probably thought all gay men had limp wrists and could cook.

"I'm one of the exceptions," I said blandly.

Rosemary opened her mouth to reply, but I was never to know what she was about to say, because the door suddenly burst open and a lean, wild-eyed man strode into the room. He had long, graying hair, was unshaven, and his shirt and trousers appeared to be cast-off clothing from a charity drive.

I assumed he was a patient, patently insane, and was about to sound the alarm, when Rosemary exclaimed, "Dad! What are you doing here?"

So this was the sometime-sculptor, Rafe Lloyd, Fenella's second husband and father of her only child. "Good morning, Mr. Lloyd," I said.

He surprised me by quite civilly replying, "Good morning. I'm afraid I don't know your name."

"Constance Sommers." Belatedly realizing I needed some semblance of authority, I added, "*Dr.* Constance Sommers."

"You're treating Rosemary?"

"Rosemary and I met for the first time this morning. We've just been having a preliminary chat."

"Oh, yeah," said Rosemary with a sneer.

There was a commotion in the hall outside, then Edward Quoint and Phoebe Murdoch, both in their pink uniforms, came hurtling through the door.

"Mr. Lloyd!" Her face scarlet, Phoebe paused to gasp for air. "Mr. Lloyd, I really must ask you to leave the premises."

Lloyd's heavy black eyebrows accentuated his scowl. "I've come here to see my daughter, you interfering bitch. Get out of here and leave us alone."

Edward Quoint, his fair hair flopping in his eyes, was incautious enough to put a large hand on Rafe Lloyd's shoulder. "If you don't—" He broke off with a cry of pain as Lloyd's elbow connected with his nose.

"Don't you dare touch me," Lloyd snarled. "Try anything else and I'll sue the pants off you, *and* the clinic, *and* bloody Thorwell. I've got the money to do it."

I had no doubt he did. His divorce from Fenella van Berg had been sweetened with several million dollars shut-up money. And it had worked: over the years Lloyd had made no public statements about his marriage or divorce, although the media had pursued him relentlessly.

Edward Quoint was bent over, hands clasped to his nose. Seeing blood leaking between his fingers, Phoebe said, "Edward, be careful not to drop blood on the carpet."

Rosemary, who'd been standing back watching the drama with an expression of keen interest, laughed unkindly. "Edward, you look just *so* dumb," she said to Quoint.

I looked around for a box of tissues, having been advised by both Estelle Decker and Peter Reynolds that all therapists kept these handy because patients so often dissolved in tears. Her statement was borne out when I located a box of tissues—pink, naturally—in the drawer of a graceful little desk.

Quoint took a wad of these with a muffled thank you, then, casting a malevolent look at Lloyd, exited with the tissues pressed to his bleeding nose.

Phoebe clasped her hands in front of her portly little body. "Mr. Lloyd, no one would argue you're entitled to see your daughter if she agrees to meet with you. However, for the protection of both our guests and their families, Easehaven Clinic has a very strict visitation protocol."

Lloyd moved until he towered over her. Leaning to put his face close to hers, he said with emphasis, "Bullshit."

I quite admired the way Phoebe responded. "Please don't try to intimidate me, Mr. Lloyd. I'm the clinic administrator, and there are guidelines I am bound to follow."

"Oh, Dad, Phoebe's okay. Leave her alone."

"Excellent advice," said Graeme Thorwell from the doorway.

Lloyd spun around. "Called the cops, have you, Thorwell?" he ground out.

"Of course not. Fenella would hardly be pleased to hear you'd caused a scene and been arrested. She'll be at Easehaven on Friday, as I suppose you know."

It was obvious from Rafe Lloyd's face he hadn't been aware his ex-wife would be visiting Australia. He darted an accusing look at his daughter. "You didn't tell me about your mother."

Rosemary's mouth trembled as her eyes filled with tears. "I didn't have a chance to tell you," she wailed. A few hiccupping breaths, then she announced, "I just want to die. To die right now!" Wracked with heavy sobs, she flung herself face down on the sofa.

Thorwell took charge. "Lloyd, it will be much better for Rosemary if you leave. Constance, will you escort Mr. Lloyd to the reception area, please? I'll join you both there as soon as possible."

I expected Lloyd to argue, but he stood irresolute for a moment, gave an unhappy, baffled look at his sobbing daughter, said, "All right, then," and almost slunk out the room.

I hurried to catch up with him. He glanced over at me, somber-faced. "Do you think you can help her, doctor?" He shook his head. "I'm just at the end of my tether, know what I mean?"

It was a bit of a shock to think Rafe Lloyd, with all his money, was asking *me* for assistance. A platitude was the best I could manage. "She's in good hands," I said soothingly.

"Thorwell, you mean? Well, he's not a quack—I'll give you that. Fenella always gets the best."

Not being quite sure how to respond, I played it safe and made a vague affirmative sound. Frowning at me, he asked, "What's your name, again?"

"Constance Sommers."

"You're a doctor?"

"Psychotherapist."

"What treatment do you recommend for my daughter?" Fortunately I didn't have to reply, as he immediately went on, "Rosemary gets depressed, she cuts herself . . . it's all a cry for help, but no one helps her."

I whipped out another platitude. "Healing takes time."

He nodded. "I suppose you're right."

We reached the reception area, which was deserted. Sinking into one of the smoky-gray chairs, Rafe Lloyd pulled out a packet of cigarettes. I was going to point out the discreet sign on the nearest low table politely thanking people for not smoking, but then I thought, *What the hell. The guy's upset enough already.*

When he offered me one, I shook my head, "No thank you, I don't smoke." As he lit his cigarette I asked if he would like tea or coffee.

"Coffee. Strong."

I went over to the reception desk, picked up the phone and punched the extension for room service, a benefit offered to patients and relatives, but conspicuously absent from the staff wing. Assured that refreshments would be provided in a few minutes, I went back to Lloyd and sank down in a chair. I hadn't noticed it before, but faint orchestral music was playing in the background.

I was feeling quite pleased with my first try at interacting with a worried relative. As long as I had a store of banal sayings, I should be able to carry it off.

Glancing over at Rafe Lloyd, I saw he was sunk in gloom. It was puzzling that he'd suddenly turned up this way, as there seemed to have been no contact between father and daughter for more than a year. Intelligence gathering wasn't infallible, of course, so perhaps the information I'd been given was flawed.

"Do you see Rosemary often?" I asked.

He raised his head. "Not often. Fenella actively discourages it." With a bitter smile he added, "She believes I'm a bad influence."

"Your daughter's an adult. Surely she can see whomever she likes."

He grunted derisively. "An adult in years, maybe. Her mother's the controlling factor in Rosemary's life, and Fenella keeps her on a short leash." He put up a hand. "Don't get me wrong. I think Fenella loves Rosemary in her own twisted way. The money it took to establish and run Easehaven and the other clinics testifies to that."

We were interrupted by the arrival of someone from the kitchen with a tray containing a coffee pot, pink mugs with *Easehaven* inscribed in blue, and an assortment of cupcakes.

Hot though it was, Rafe Lloyd gulped down the contents of the mug I handed him, then leaned over for a refill. "I may have caused Rosemary more harm than good, barging my way in here this morning."

"As a therapist," I said, squashing my inclination to smile at this self-description, "I do feel Rosemary's relationship with you is a very important one."

"Tell Fenella that, will you?" He absently dabbed at a spot of coffee he'd just managed to splash on his crumpled shirt.

"I'll do that. If I may ask, why did you come here today?"

"Dr. Bradley."

I hoped my astonishment didn't show. "Dr. Norah Bradley?"

Why would Rafe Lloyd have anything to do with Norah Bradley? She'd been the psychiatrist who'd given evidence at the inquest inquiring into the car accident that had killed her patient, Anita Hutching, and two others. As far as I knew, Dr. Bradley had never treated Rosemary Lloyd.

A picture of her rose in my mind. I'd studied her file, along with the other members of staff at Easehaven. She was about my height, with an oval, serene face. Her dark brown hair was pulled back in an old-fashioned bun. I remembered the photograph had shown her long, graceful hands. Norah Bradley had come from a family where a much-beloved brother had committed suicide, hanging himself in a holiday cabin. Norah Bradley, deeply marked by this, had become a psychiatrist, specializing in the treatment of suicidal teenagers. She had written many papers on the subject, and was an acknowledged authority.

Rafe Lloyd said. "Is she here?"

"I don't think so. Would you like me to check?" I was pleased to be given this excuse to ask a direct question about Dr. Bradley without anyone wondering why I was interested in someone I'd never met.

Lloyd poured himself a third coffee. "She's been my eyes and ears, you see, keeping me informed. After my daughter's last breakdown, Fenella froze me out. I couldn't find out anything about Rosemary's treatment or how she was doing."

"And Dr. Bradley supplied the information?"

"She's very well paid for it. It's a business arrangement, but I like to think Dr. Bradley is actually fond of Rosemary and cares what happens to her." He put down his mug with a thump. "When she didn't contact me on schedule, I had my personal assistant call Easehaven and ask for her. Got the run around. First Dr. Bradley wasn't available, then a couple of calls later, the story changed. Now she was taking a couple of weeks off."

"What did you think had happened?"

He shrugged. "That someone—probably Thorwell doing Fenella's dirty work—had found out how I was getting information about Rosemary, and had threatened to fire Dr. Bradley if she kept it up. I decided to drive up from Sydney and see for myself what the situation was."

Seeing a flash of whiter than white in the hallway, I realized Graeme Thorwell was approaching, his hands rammed into the pockets of his pristine coat. I got up hastily, saying, "Here's Dr. Thorwell. I'll leave you to discuss Rosemary with him, while I check on Dr. Bradley for you."

I skipped off to the administration office before Thorwell reached us. Teena was on the phone. "My husband," she said, ending the call. "He's in Gosford Hospital."

"Nothing serious, I hope."

"Colon cancer."

There wasn't any good reply to that. I said, "I'm so sorry."

Teena said brightly, "How can I help you, Dr. Sommers?"

I said, quite accurately, "I have a query from a patient's father about Dr. Bradley. He'd like to see her. Is she here today?"

Teena maneuvered her wheelchair over to the computer screen. "Norah Bradley? Think she's away at the moment. Some family emergency."

"He's very anxious to speak with her. Do you think she might be available?"

Teena's fingers danced over the keys. "Yes, see here," she said, pointing. "Norah Bradley's taken compassionate leave. A death in the family."

"When will she be back?"

Teena peered a the screen. "Odd. It doesn't say."

I turned as Phoebe's tight English tones inquired, "Can I be of some help?"

"Dr. Sommers was just asking about Norah Bradley," said Teena.

"Indeed?" Phoebe's eyebrows rose above blue eyes not half as deep in hue as Graeme Thorwell's contact lenses.

"It's Rafe Lloyd," I said. "I'm not sure why, but he wants to speak with Dr. Bradley. He asked me to find out if she's scheduled to be on duty today."

"Rafe Lloyd is asking?" she said with distaste. "After what he did to Edward's face, I don't feel at all disposed to be of help to him in any way whatsoever."

"I understand that." I put a touch of frost in my tone. After all, I was a doctor, wasn't I? Given half a chance, I reckoned this pocket-size despot would boss anyone around, whoever they might be. It was time to make a stand. "The fact remains, however, Mr. Lloyd has asked for information I gather pertains to his daughter. I don't believe we can refuse to provide it."

Phoebe's small, red mouth compressed itself into a hard line. I glanced at Teena, who appeared to be holding her breath, waiting for the storm to break.

Phoebe said with cold emphasis, "Dr. Bradley is not, at this moment, available. The date of her return is uncertain. It's unfortunate if this information fails to satisfy Mr. Lloyd, but that's all that can be said."

"Who died?"

Phoebe looked momentarily startled. "Died?"

"Teena's records indicate Dr. Bradley's on compassionate leave because someone died."

Phoebe's patience with me was rapidly wearing thin. "I know nothing about Norah Bradley's personal life, nor do I want to. She's not available at the moment. Frankly, that's all I need to know." She glowered at me. "That's all *anyone* needs to know."

I didn't challenge Phoebe over the fact that yesterday she'd boasted how Dr. Thorwell insisted she know every detail about staff and patients.

"Okay, I'll tell Mr. Lloyd that," I said, suddenly agreeable. "Oh, and I do have something you need to know."

Phoebe glared at me. "Yes?" It was clear her displeasure with me was acute.

"I'll be away from Easehaven for a couple of hours this afternoon. I've got some personal business to attend to—getting a cell phone, buying a few things . . ."

She nodded permission. "Very well. When you're ready to go, ask Sean to bring your car around for you."

"Can't I get it from the garage myself? I scoped out where it was yesterday afternoon."

"If you wish, but in that case please notify Teena when you're leaving. At Easehaven we like to keep track of staff movements in case of emergencies."

"I'll do that," I said, cooperation itself, while thinking, *I bet you'll search my room once you know I've gone.*

CHAPTER EIGHT

"Zena?"

"Connie. How lovely to hear from you."

"I'm using a public phone."

"I see that."

Of course Cynthia-Zena could see that. The point of origin of all incoming calls would be displayed on a monitor in front of her. Visualizing the light from the screen emphasizing the planes of her angular face, I said, "Are you chomping on carrots, perhaps?" I was still getting used to the idea she was a vegetarian.

Imperturbable as always, she said, "Not at the moment. Are you secure?"

I glanced around the food court at the shopping mall. My phone was at one end of five set in a row. A clear plastic hood over each was supposed to provide privacy, but I could still catch snatches of the teenage girl's conversation next to me. She was telling someone in eyebrow-raising detail what she and her boyfriend had done last night.

I'd chosen the food court area because it was crowded, noisy, and there was constant movement of people coming and going. It would be impossible for anyone to get close to overhear my conversation, unless they were pretending to use the next phone, and I was absolutely sure the girl on that instrument was oblivious to me or anything else around her.

"I'm secure," I said, my hand cupped so no one could read my lips. A concealed directional microphone was a possibility, but I kept my voice low and relied on the ambient noise to drown my words.

"Connie, I've information for you, but let's start with what you've got for me."

Our conversation was being recorded at ASIO, so Zena didn't have to make notes. First, I gave her the number of my new cell phone. It was for emergency use only. Within a few minutes technicians would make sure that outgoing and incoming calls to that number would be automatically re-routed so it would be impossible to establish where calls had originated.

In this particular undercover assignment such refinements were probably not necessary. Scans of Easehaven had shown no tapped lines, no electronic cloaking systems—in fact, no sophisticated spying devices of any kind. But, after all, Graeme Thorwell essentially had nothing to hide: he was working within accepted psychiatric procedures. And whatever had been done to Anita Hutching and Josetta Wilson to turn them into human weapons could not have been perceived by physical means. It had all been in their heads.

"Okay, Zena, this is what I've got." As briefly as possible, I explained Madison Petrie was in the secured section of the clinic, heavily sedated. I was working on the problem of how to get to see her. I described Rosemary Lloyd's almost certainly unrequited passion for Thorwell, and mentioned the negative effect the news of Fenella van Berg's unexpected visit was having on her daughter. I pointed out that Fenella's imminent arrival had forced me to use the

76

fallback story that it had been Kym Browne who'd recommended me. I detailed how Rafe Lloyd had caused a ruckus by forcing his way in, and then how he'd possibly broken Edward Quoint's nose. I told Zena how Rafe Lloyd had been paying Norah Bradley to covertly report to him on Rosemary's progress. And last, Norah Bradley was supposed to be on compassionate leave because an unnamed family member had died, but I suspected this was merely a story to cover her disappearance.

"When I went back to tell Lloyd about Dr. Bradley," I said, "Thorwell had gone, and Lloyd was pacing up and down, smoking. I gave him the news Norah Bradley was away because of family problems. Lloyd was annoyed she'd failed to tell him she would be on leave, and asked me to instruct her to call him the moment she returned."

"Here's my feedback on these items," said Zena briskly. "Regarding Madison Petrie, a member of her family will turn up, demanding to see her. As far as Fenella's ex-assistant is concerned, I'll make sure she's neutralized. And Norah Bradley? We'll investigate and report later."

"Okay," I said, "your turn. Enlighten me."

Zena had three items. I asked a few clarifying questions, then hung up. I pretended to make another call while checking out everything around me. Nothing seemed out of place. I didn't think I'd been followed, but even if I had been, I'd done nothing suspicious, except maybe using a public phone when I'd just gone to the trouble of getting a cell phone. But perhaps I hadn't been able to get a clear signal at this location, so had used a landline instead.

It was standard practice to be so cautious, even though everything pointed to the fact that Dr. Constance Sommers had been accepted for whom she appeared to be. No one had any reason to think otherwise.

As I shopped for a few things I did actually need, like shampoo and hand cream, I mulled over what Zena had just told me. The action to be taken on the items I'd raised with her was clear. An agent claiming to be a relative of the CIA's agent, Madison Petrie, would be coming to visit her. Kym Browne, Fenella's erstwhile assistant, would be isolated in some way so no one could contact her with questions about her recommendation of Constance Sommers. As far as Dr. Norah Bradley was concerned, the story she was on leave because of a bereavement would be investigated.

The new information Zena had given me was disturbing. Another suicide bombing had been linked to one of Thorwell's clinics. The delay in making the connection was because Patsy Kimble's body had not been identified until British authorities had been alerted by Josetta Wilson's assassination of Senator O'Neven in Australia, and had begun to check data bases in the States for missing young women fitting the description of their suspect who had been treated at one of the Thorwell clinics.

Patsy Kimble had been a patient at the Houston clinic nine months before, while Graeme Thorwell had been in residence there. After checking herself out, Patsy had taken a flight to London and disappeared for a few days. She'd reappeared at a huge peace rally, where she'd embraced a noted scientist who'd just completed an impassioned speech against nuclear arms. Her last words had been picked up by an open microphone. "I am come to you," Patsy Kimble had said just before she detonated the bomb strapped to her body.

And now the words Josetta Wilson had spoken had been deciphered by sound engineers. "I am come to you," she had said to Senator O'Neven.

Two angels of death, using the same words. It made me shiver.

Zena's last piece of information was quite surprising. "Our forensic accountants," Zena said, "have uncovered interesting information about Daphne Webster. It seems she's salted away a great deal of money, more than she could possibly have made by legal means. And she's hidden it in very sophisticated ways, so she's obviously had professional help."

"We're talking how much?"

"In point of fact, millions."

I'd actually gasped. The news that Daphne was a millionaire was unsettling, to say the least. So why was she working at Easehaven?

"Zena, are you sure? Maybe she won the lottery."

"There's no record of her winning a lottery, or having a rich uncle die, or anything of that nature. You need to get close to this woman, find out what you can." She'd chuckled. "You have my encouragement to use any reasonable means to get her to talk." She'd added, her voice suddenly serious, "Constance, be careful. The CIA's agent has already been deactivated in some way. I wouldn't want anything to happen to you."

"Any idea how she got all this money?"

"The consensus here is that Daphne Webster's been paid off. She's part of a contract killing conspiracy."

No, not Daphne. I hardly knew her, but couldn't accept her in that role.

I drove back to Easehaven and parked my car in the same place I'd found it in before. I was charmed to see that while I'd been out someone had affixed my name to the wall to indicate this was my personal parking spot.

The vehicles in the extensive underground garage ranged from monstrous four wheel drives—Constance, of course, would call them SUVs—to sleek little sports cars. There were also a number of utilitarian vehicles like my rental, suitable for getting from point A to B, but totally uninspiring otherwise. I made a mental note to make noises about buying a car, as no one would expect me to drive a rental for long.

Checking out other designated spots, I found Phoebe was driving a black BMW and Graeme Thorwell a silver Bentley. Out of curiosity, I wandered along until I located Daphne's name. She might have millions salted away, but she hadn't spent much on her transport—it was a rather battered red Toyota SUV.

When I went to the administration office to advise Teena I'd returned to the Easehaven fold, she whipped her wheelchair around to look at me with an expression I initially had trouble deciphering. When I realized it was admiration with a touch of wonder, I said, "What's up, Teena?"

"It's Dr. Thorwell . . . Graeme . . ."

"Yes?"

"He's inviting you to a private dinner tonight in his rooms."

From her breathless tone, I gathered at this news I was supposed to stagger back, pressing my hand to my heart. I said, "Is that a big deal?"

Obviously surprised I'd asked, Teena said, "Yes, it *is* a big deal, Constance. It's extremely rare for Graeme to have his evening meal anywhere but with the staff and guests in the dining room. Of course he does have private dinners with Ms. van Berg and certain VIPs, but otherwise . . ." She spread her hands.

"I guess I should be honored, then."

Teena handed me a square, sealed envelope, saying, "Phoebe's noted down the menu, in case you have any dietary restrictions or allergies. If you do, please tell her immediately."

"No allergies, no restrictions."

"And she's included instructions about the time you should arrive and the dress requirements."

"You're kidding me! Dress requirements?"

Teena shared my grin. "A bit over the top, you think?"

"A bit." I peered into the adjoining office, which was Phoebe's domain. Naturally it was both larger and better furnished than Teena's area. Ascertaining she wasn't there, I asked, "What does Phoebe think of this invitation?"

Teena looked around conspiratorially, then dropped her voice to say, "Actually, quite miffed. She's often in Graeme's rooms, of course, discussing various things to do with the running of the place, but Phoebe's never had an invitation to dinner."

The more I thought about this, the less I liked it. What in the hell was Thorwell up to? Did he have a romantic dinner in mind where he'd put the hard word on me? Surely not, unless he had a death wish. I could well imagine Rosemary would have his guts for gaiters if she thought he was interested in someone else.

Or perhaps in some way Thorwell had suspicions about Constance Sommers, and intended to lull me into a false sense of security so he could catch me out. Two could play that game: maybe he'd drink as heavily as he had last night and I'd be the one to pump him for information.

I went back to my room to drop off my purchases. It was almost a relief to see that my belongings had been searched. Before leaving I'd memorized the alignments of several different items, knowing it would be impossible for an intruder to return every single thing exactly to its original position. Our rooms were cleaned once a week and the beds changed. This meant that several people would have master keys to unlock doors. Whoever had been through my possessions—and I was betting it was Phoebe—would now know I apparently had absolutely nothing to hide.

Late this afternoon I was scheduled to have a session with my first patient, Nat Scott. He was a fifteen-year-old who'd tried to burn down the family home. He'd narrowly avoided detention in a youth facility, in part because his parents arranged to admit him to Easehaven for treatment. It went without saying the family had money, as this place didn't come cheap.

He'd only been in the clinic for a couple of days, so the only things in his file were preliminary items, including the psychiatric evidence given at his children's court hearing by, I was fascinated to see, Dr. Norah Bradley. His entry interview at Easehaven had been carried out by Graeme Thorwell himself.

I went to the designated consultation room with some trepidation, worrying about how I'd perform as a therapist. I didn't think I'd be able to keep an impartial view of proceedings, as I had a distinct bias against arsonists.

The room, needless to say, was pink. It was simply furnished with comfortable chairs. A vase of red and white roses shared a low table with the ubiquitous box of tissues.

Ever-smiling Nurse Gretchen Hamilton, apparently continuing to be as delighted with life as she had been at the function last night, effervesced her way into the room with Nat Scott. "I've just been telling Nat how *very* lucky he is to have *you* heading his ease team!"

Oh, groan. Ease team? "Thank you, Gretchen."

"Always a total pleasure! Nat, I'll be back to collect you in exactly fifty minutes. You be good, now!"

Nat Scott was an earnest young man with a habit of tapping his stubby fingers on his thighs. He sat silent for a few moments, then said, "Where's Dr. Bradley?"

"She's away, I'm afraid. You'll have to make do with me."

"Oh, okay."

I figured I could do little harm by encouraging him to do the talking, and might do some good, so I said, "Tell me about yourself," and spent most of the allotted time listening, jotting down what I hoped were coherent notes—Peter had drilled me in that area—and now and then throwing in a mild comment or question.

It was astonishing how much Nat freely told me about his family dynamics, his relationships with his parents and sister, and his lack of close friends. I began to see him as an isolated, unhappy young man, not merely a destructive arsonist. Unprompted, he even brought up the subject, explaining how he'd set the fire after making sure no one was in the house. When he'd been sure it was fully ablaze, he went outside and joined the neighbors and passing people who were rapidly assembling to view the drama, waiting with them while fire engines, sirens wailing, had arrived.

"Mmmmm," I said, "and what were you feeling, Nat?"

Hey! I was sounding like a real therapist.

"I suppose I felt pleased and sad at the same time, you know?"

82

I tried another, "Mmmmm."

"Like, I was pleased I had the power to make something happen, but I was sad about the house."

I'd read that there was often a sexual element in arson, but looking at Nat's adolescent form, I decided I wasn't game to go in that direction. "Tell me about power," I said. That was enough to get Nat rambling on for the last fifteen minutes of our session together.

Punctual to the second, Gretchen put her head around the door and smiled at us. "Time's up, Nat."

I was really quite touched when he said, "Thanks, doc. Like, I feel a lot better, you know? Talking about everything and all. So I'll see you tomorrow then?"

"I don't have a firm schedule yet, but I'm sure we'll talk again."

I spent a few minutes tidying up my notes. A briefing meeting was held each morning so medical staff could report on patients' progress, or otherwise, in the past twenty-four hours. I hadn't been required to go to this morning's briefing, but tomorrow I'd have to put in an appearance and say something intelligent about Nat Scott.

I gathered up my things and left in search of a strong cup of tea. Outside the room I ran into Edward Quoint. His nose was heavily taped, and obviously painfully swollen. "Broken?" I asked.

He ran a hand through his floppy hair. I wondered how he could stand having it falling into his eyes all the time. "Thanks for asking, Constance. Only badly bruised." He added with a rueful smile, "I should learn to duck. As you know, in psychiatry you get into the odd free-for-all with disturbed people, but I wasn't expecting a parent to assault me. My mistake."

On an impulse, I said, "Do you know Norah Bradley?"

"Of course. Why?"

"I've just been with a patient, Nat Scott, who asked where she was. And this morning Rafe Lloyd had the same question."

Although Edward Quoint's face darkened at the mention of his attacker, he didn't comment, but answered my question quite openly. "A couple of weeks ago Norah up and disappeared. I think Phoebe said it was a family emergency of some sort. No idea where she is, but for all I know, Norah could stroll in tomorrow."

"What happened to the cases she was handling?" To avoid this sounding too inquisitive, I added quickly, "I'm asking because I've ended up treating Nat Scott, who was to be her patient. I'm just wondering who else is in the pipeline."

"Norah did a lot of work in the Sanctuary section, so I wouldn't know anything about her cases there."

"Sanctuary? You mean the maximum security area for violent patients?"

Quoint shook his forefinger at me. "Constance, you've got to stop calling them patients. You know the Easehaven term is guest." He grinned. "I'll have to report you, if you don't change your ways."

"Forgive me. I'll rephrase. Is this another name for the security area for violent guests?"

"It's part of it, but separate." He pantomimed looking over his shoulder to make sure he couldn't be overheard. "It's called the Sanctuary Project," he said in a stage whisper. "If you ask me, it's something to do with the government. Top secret."

Making my skepticism plain, I said, "Oh, come on, Edward, like what?"

"Like I don't know. Truth serums, maybe. Whatever, it doesn't pay to be too interested. I asked Norah once what she was doing there, and she clammed up. And a day later Phoebe chewed me out for asking questions about things outside my area. Made it clear I'd be out of a job if I kept it up. So I lost interest fast."

"You're telling me about it."

"Ah, yes," he said, "but you're an esteemed doctor, not a lowly nurse like yours truly. If you ask questions, you'll get answers."

I thought that highly unlikely.

❦

Phoebe's written instructions were to arrive at Thorwell's rooms at seven-thirty sharp. I was to wear something suitable for a formal dinner. She would call my room at precisely seven-twenty to make sure I was on schedule. This woman would give Genghis Khan a run for his money.

I decided I couldn't go wrong with the standard black dress. Daphne knocked on my door while I was deciding what jewelry to wear. She came in and sat on the bed while I finished dressing.

"At Easehaven scarcely two days," she said with a sardonic grin, "and already having intimate private dinners with the lord of the manor. I call that a meteoric rise."

"I call it tiresome."

"But Graeme's so handsome."

"Is he? I hadn't noticed."

"Well, he'll notice you, Connie. You're looking terrific."

"It always pays to impress the boss," I said.

Daphne raised an eyebrow. "Graeme's not really the boss."

"No? Fenella van Berg is?"

"Maybe."

I laughed. "You're not telling me Phoebe runs the show?"

"After you leave Graeme's scintillating company this evening, come back to my room for a nightcap. I'll spill the beans then."

"You're luring me to your room with promises of secrets?"

She smiled. "Just knock three times."

The phone rang. It was Phoebe. I was short with her. "Phoebe, for heaven's sake, you don't need to check on me. I'm a punctual woman, okay?"

Dinner was served in Thorwell's private sitting room, which was directly entered from the hallway. One corner had been set up as a dining area. I had expected the room's sumptuous furnishings and the elegance of the table-settings and glassware. For some reason I didn't expect the candles on the table. This romantic touch was more than unwelcome. Fending off Thorwell's advances without totally alienating him would be a wearisome task.

The young woman who'd assisted at the function last night was serving our meal, and as she placed our appetizers on the table, Thorwell said, "Constance, let me give you a quick tour before we sit down."

I already knew the layout, but a floor plan didn't even suggest the sleek luxury of the apartment. I pleased Thorwell by openly admiring his study, making appreciative noises over his black-and-white marble bathroom with a sunken bath quite big enough for a minor orgy, and praising the beautiful patio and garden outside his bedroom.

The bedroom itself I thought better not to comment upon, although he was at pains to point out the beauty of the hand-woven bedspread on the king-size bed.

When we went back to the dining table, the candles were lit, the main light extinguished, and for the moment, our server had disappeared. The only thing missing was soft music. To my hidden amusement, Thorwell immediately strode over to an elaborate sound system, punched a button, and filled the room with the requisite background of syrupy orchestral sounds.

As he filled my wine glass, he said, "I was impressed by the way you dealt with Rosemary Lloyd yesterday."

"You were?"

"To initiate communication by using her past experiences with me was an excellent idea. I must comment, however, that the plastic surgery Rosemary mentioned me having was just a minor nose job." Electric smile. "I wouldn't want you to think I was vain."

As Thorwell hadn't been present when Rosemary and I had had this particular conversation, I said, "Graeme, I can think of only three ways you could know what we discussed: one, Rosemary told you afterwards; two, you had your ear pressed against the door eavesdropping; three, there's a hidden recording device in the room."

"The third alternative. All consultations are recorded as part of the comprehensive treatment documentation we maintain for each of our guests."

Constance Sommers, psychotherapist, would protest at not being informed of this secret taping, so I frowned and said sharply, "I wished you had told me about this surveillance."

"Would it have made any difference to what you said and did?"

"I don't imagine so."

"Then no harm done." He paused for a gulp of wine. I sipped mine. After a moment, he said, "Constance, you will have noted how Rosemary has become overly dependent upon me."

He paused, perhaps to give me time to consider how impossible it would be for any female patient to avoid this fate.

"Mmmmm," I said, figuring this noncommittal response had worked for me this afternoon in Nat Scott's session, so why not here?

"This attachment," he went on, "though understandable, severely limits the effectiveness of my work with her. It's my intention to have you replace me as her primary therapist. I, of course, will still be involved, but marginally."

"I suspect Rosemary will object strenuously."

"Be that as it may."

I nodded acquiescence. "I'm willing to try."

On the one hand this was a helpful development, because if I were to be treating Rosemary I would be close to the center of action in Easehaven. On the other hand, Rosemary herself was very likely to reject me in the most emphatic manner, and I doubted I had the skills to turn her around.

"I'm puzzled," I said. "Why choose me? You said yourself Rosemary didn't relate well to woman."

"True, but overcoming this is a vital element in her treatment. It will be valuable for you to meet Rosemary's mother on Friday. I'm sure direct observation of the dynamics between mother and daughter will be of interest to you."

The dinner proceeded uneventfully. Our server reappeared with the main course, Beef Wellington. I wondered what Zena, being a vegetarian, would think of this chunk of rare steak. Not much, I guessed. I imagined her sitting opposite me. The candlelight would flatter her. I looked critically at Thorwell. He was smoothly handsome, true, but under his glossy surface there was something ugly.

"Constance," he said, smiling winningly across the table, "I've taken the liberty of reviewing your career and professional experience, and I must say I'm most impressed at your expertise in hypnotherapy."

"Really?" I said. "It's quite boring. They keep falling asleep while I'm talking to them."

Thorwell looked blank, then laughed a little too hard. "Very good, Constance. Like me, you understand a sense of humor is essential when dealing with the human psyche."

"If you don't laugh, you'll cry."

"Just so, just so."

He busied himself topping up our wine glasses, although mine was more than half full. His was almost empty. I couldn't help wondering if it were more than Fenella van Berg's imminent arrival that was driving him to drink.

"I see in your work history you spent some time at the Brindesi Institute," he said.

This was my cue to achieve the tricky task of saying little and implying much. "I'm afraid I signed a confidentiality agreement, Graeme. I'd love to discuss the details of my work at the Institute, but I'm precluded from doing so."

"No details, but in general terms, perhaps?" He sent me a charming, you-can-tell-me smile. "I've long been intrigued by the Brindesi Institute. Much of their work is for foreign governments, I believe."

I played with my glass. "I suppose that's common knowledge, so I've no problem in confirming it," I said. "However, as much of the Institute's research is at the cutting edge of psychological manipulation, you'll appreciate I can say little more."

He leaned forward confidingly. "Constance, it's an area in which I have the keenest interest."

I looked down demurely at my wine. "The research did push the ethical envelope . . ."

"Sometimes barriers have to be broken to achieve great things," Thorwell declared. He added, with a laugh, "You can't make an omelet without breaking a few psychological eggs, as one might say!"

I hid my disgust at his attitude with a polite smile. "The good of the many outweighs the welfare of the few?" I said.

"Exactly. I see we think alike." His smile faded, to be replaced with a solemn expression. "Constance, what I'm going to tell you is confidential, deeply confidential."

The way he kept repeating my name was clearly to establish closeness. I hardly knew this pompous guy, I didn't like or trust him, and he was really starting to irritate me. "You intrigue me," I purred.

"Rather like the Brindesi Institute, here at Easehaven we've been developing special projects."

It was my turn to lean forward, my expression one of intense interest. "Please tell me more."

"We're examining states of altered consciousness. I must assure you this is not merely research for research's sake—there is a national security component."

"You're working for the Australian government?" I sounded quite impressed.

"Indirectly. Constance, not a word of this must leave this room. Perhaps even more than the Brindesi Institute, our work demands total secrecy."

"Of course, Graeme."

With an apparent change of subject, he said, "I know you've been asking about Norah Bradley's case load."

Edward Quoint and I had been in the hallway, away from any recording equipment in the consulting room. No one had been close enough to overhear us. That meant Quoint had repeated our conversation. I doubted he'd told Graeme Thorwell direct, so Phoebe would be my best guess.

I said with a faint shrug, "I've inherited Nat Scott, teenage arsonist. I was wondering whom else I might pick up from Dr. Bradley's list."

Thorwell's expression was grave. "Unfortunately I've just been informed Norah will not be returning to Easehaven for personal reasons I'm not at liberty to reveal."

I nodded, all alert attention.

"Norah will be very much missed," he went on, shaking his head. "She's been involved in vital research work for us in this covert area I mentioned." His handsome face quite compelling in the candlelight, he went on, "I was wondering if you'd be willing to pick up the slack."

"Norah was using hypnotherapy in her research?"

"She was using a whole range of psychiatric strategies. Hypnotism was one of them."

There was an urgent knocking at the door. "Graeme! Graeme!"

Obviously furious to be interrupted, he swore to himself, got to his feet, strode to the door, and ripped it open. "What?"

I caught a glimpse of Phoebe's distraught face as she looked up at him. "It's Rosemary. She's tried to kill herself."

CHAPTER NINE

I knocked three times on Daphne's door. She opened it almost immediately. "Come in." She was wearing a black T-shirt sans bra, faded pale blue jeans and had bare feet. Her toenails were painted crimson.

I looked around, thinking, *This woman has a couple of million dollars, so why is she here?* The answers came immediately. *More money. Power. Radical political beliefs. Or all of the above.*

Daphne's room was almost identical to mine, but she had two chairs, I noted. My room had only one. "You've got two chairs," I said.

She grinned at my accusatory tone. "I purloined the extra one from Norah Bradley's room this evening. I suppose you've heard. She isn't coming back to the clinic."

"Graeme told me over dinner. He said she wasn't returning for personal reasons."

"He said that, did he?"

"You don't think it's true?"

"Graeme's often careless with the truth." She said this with an offhand disdain, as though the head of Easehaven was of little account. That brought me back to the reason I was here—to find out who Daphne believed was really in charge of the clinic.

She motioned for me to sit down and I automatically chose the chair giving me the best view of the door and window.

"You've got a choice of wine or vodka," she said. "I've ice, if you go for the hard stuff."

I'd rationed my alcohol intake at dinner to two glasses, my usual limit. Although I didn't really feel like more alcohol now, to be sociable I said, "Wine, please."

"Coming right up."

I watched her with pleasure, and, to be truthful, with a pulse of desire. Daphne's slim, smoothly-muscled body was alluring, and Zena had obliquely given me the green light. I visualized kissing Daphne's full mouth, running my fingers through her springy black hair . . .

"Rosemary Lloyd tried to kill herself, I hear," she said, handing me a glass. Pulling the chair closer to mine, she sat opposite me and took a sip of her vodka on the rocks. I was very aware our knees were almost touching.

The news had certainly got out fast. I'd just come from Rosemary's bedroom. She was sedated and under constant observation. Thorwell had sworn everyone involved to secrecy, emphasizing that Fenella had specifically requested that any such incident was to be treated with the utmost discretion. I recalled Edward Quoint nodding enthusiastically as Thorwell spoke.

"My guess is Edward Quoint spilled the beans," I said.

"As I'm head of nursing, Graeme called a few minutes ago to bring me up to speed. Edward called right after him, making sure I'd heard. He loves to be the one with the juicy gossip. When something interesting happens around here, it's a tossup who broadcasts it first, Edward or Phoebe."

"This afternoon Edward was telling me about something called Sanctuary Project."

"He's got a real bee in his bonnet about that. Can't stand it that he isn't involved."

"Are you involved?"

"Of course. It's a confidential undertaking. Very hush hush."

I was debating whether to tell her Thorwell had been discussing my participation in the project, when Daphne said, "Ultimately someone like Rosemary Lloyd will be helped by what we're doing in Sanctuary Project."

"What exactly *are* you doing?"

"Behavior modification."

I tried to give an impression of subtle disappointment at this information. "Is that all? It hardly seems worthy of such secrecy."

"Connie, I'm not talking about commonplace methods of persuasion, but I afraid I can't go into details. I've signed a comprehensive non-disclosure document with very nasty financial and career penalties if I break confidentiality."

"I hope there are new treatments in the pipeline for Rosemary," I said in heartfelt tones, "since it looks like Dr. Thorwell's set on handing her over to me."

"I don't think Rosemary's case is all that complicated," said Daphne. "Tonight she only nicked her wrists. It wasn't a fair dinkum suicide attempt."

"She's tried it before, hasn't she?" I asked.

"If Rosemary had ever been genuinely trying to kill herself in the past, she wouldn't be around now," said Daphne dryly. "She'd be pushing up daisies."

"Too true."

"Her mother's about to arrive and monopolize Graeme. Under the circumstances, why not generate a little extra attention with a suicide attempt?"

"So that's all it is?" I asked. "Attention getting?"

"Do you think I sound unsympathetic? I'm not. Sure, it's easy to mock a poor little rich girl like Rosemary Lloyd, who's never worked a day in her life and can have every material thing she wants. But I doubt she's ever been happy. She wouldn't recognize happiness if it trotted up and punched her on the nose."

"I think that's a mixed metaphor. And if it isn't, it should be."

Daphne regarded me with a knowing smile. "The mixed metaphor is you, Connie."

"What do you mean by that?"

She leaned forward and put a hand on my thigh.

"You give one message and mean another."

I had no fear Daphne Webster could know anything about my real identity, but still, I felt a thrill, and not just of alarm. "Are you trying to seduce me?"

"Not trying. I am."

It was growing hot in the room. "I'm impervious," I said. She laughed.

Heat ran from her hand up into me like a shaft of warm light. "I'm a psychotherapist," I said, "and so understand my carnal impulses are merely conditioned reflexes." I looked at her mouth.

She said, "As a psychotherapist, you know how damaging it can be to suppress one's deeper feelings."

I sighed. "That's the trouble with you psychiatric nurses—you know too much."

She put her free hand on my other thigh. Wow!

I must have said it aloud, because she repeated, "Wow, indeed," and bent forward until our lips touched.

"I've got a question," I said.

Her tongue flickered along my lips. "Uh-huh?"

"How did you get into Norah Bradley's room?"

Daphne drew back. "My God," she said, "you do ask the weirdest questions."

"You said you got a chair out of her room. How did you get in?"

94

"Master key. Borrowed it from housekeeping."

"So someone could burst in on us any moment, using housekeeping's master key?"

Daphne laughed as she got to her feet. "You're such a worrywart." Grabbing her chair, she strode across to the door and jammed the back under the doorknob. "Happy now?"

"Almost ecstatic, but you did promise to tell me one more thing."

Daphne folded her arms and regarded me with a quizzical smile. "I was hoping to get much better acquainted with you, Connie, but I find myself answering twenty questions instead. Are you playing hard to get, or are you just not interested?"

"I'm interested," I said with perfect truth, "but fair's fair. You lured me into your room with the promise you'd tell me who the real boss is around here." I paused for a cheeky grin. "It's for my career, you understand. How can I kowtow to the right person if I don't know who he or she is?"

"And is that it? If I tell you can we go on where we just left off?"

"Absolutely."

"Harry Gerlich."

"You're joking," I said. "The antisocial guy who didn't succumb to my sunny smile?"

"The very one." She opened her arms. "Question answered: payment required."

It was a price I was willing to pay. She felt as she looked, coiled tension in a strong, agile body. I was super fit, as before every assignment I trained body and mind to give me the edge both physically and mentally. Even so, I'd met my match here. Daphne had kept her athlete's strength and flexibility.

She was thrilling, she was challenging. Our combat flooded me with fire, devouring me until all my control and logic burned away.

"You'll kill me," I gasped, vibrating beneath her hands. I seized her, wrestled with her, came with her.

Wet, breathless, we sank into a quiescent embrace.

"Who are you?" Daphne whispered.

I turned my head and gently bit her shoulder. "Constance Sommers, psychotherapist."

"You're not like any therapist I've ever known."

"No? Better in bed?"

She laughed softly. "Oh, that too, but what I mean is, you don't take yourself too seriously."

I met her thoughtful gaze with a tingle of disquiet. The danger wasn't making love with the enemy—it was letting her get so close to the essential me. "It's all an act," I assured her. "Underneath I'm appallingly full of myself."

CHAPTER TEN

The next morning, Thursday, I came to breakfast feeling rather tired, which was not surprising, considering the hours of athletic activity I engaged in the night before, and the little sleep I managed to snatch after I'd gone back to my room.

Daphne was on early shift, so had eaten early, and although Edward Quoint waved to me, I pretended I didn't see him and went to a table in a corner to eat a solitary breakfast.

I was just finishing when Harry Gerlich approached. "A word, Dr. Sommers."

"Of course, Dr. Gerlich."

Repressing an atavistic shudder of distaste, I motioned him to sit. He was no more prepossessing this morning than he'd been at the function on Tuesday night. He was a weedy man, with hunched shoulders and greasy, gray-streaked hair. As I'd noticed before, the shadow of his beard showed through his pallid skin.

He was carrying a leather folder, which he put on the table in front of him. Then he swiveled his head around to survey the room. Apparently satisfied all was in order, without haste he took reading glasses from the top pocket of his white coat and polished them carefully with a pink tissue. Setting the glasses on his nose, he opened the folder. I recognized pages from my resume.

His black eyes seemed not to blink. "I do have some questions about your career and experience," he said.

"You do? I believe Dr. Thorwell is quite satisfied with my qualifications."

"Graeme has recommended you for work on Sanctuary. It is a project of great importance, and largely my responsibility. I'm sure you'll understand the necessity for scrupulous care in the selection of staff."

"I do, Dr. Gerlich," I said with as much sincerity as I could muster. I checked my watch. "I'm due at the morning briefing shortly."

"You're excused from that today."

For the next hour Gerlich grilled me about where I'd been and what I'd done, particularly in North America, where I'd spent the most illustrious part of my career. My resume had included articles by Constance Sommers published in journals, as well as transcripts of addresses and lectures to various professional associations. I'd included copies of some of these purported items, which had been dummied up from genuine material written by other professionals. To ASIO, plagiarism, at least in the national interest, was perfectly acceptable. None of the journals was likely to be in Easehaven's library, but if someone went to the trouble to do an Internet search, some holes could appear in my story. The gamble was that no one would do this, and the astonishing gullibility of the majority of employers who rarely checked the stories of highly qualified applicants, gave me hope that the odds were on my side.

Several times I silently thanked Zena and Peter for the ruthless drilling they'd given me over every point of Constance's supposed career, and Dr. Jeffrey, Peter and Estelle Decker's insistence that I learn the daily ins and outs of a therapist's professional life.

"The Brindesi Institute," said Gerlich. "You were doing classified work there?"

"As I explained to Dr. Thorwell, for legal reasons I'm unable to discuss details of my time at the Institute."

"I understand that," he said impatiently. "You'll be required to sign a similar confidentiality agreement with Easehaven. What I require is a general outline of your research." He gave me a wintry smile. "I believe you can satisfy my questions without contravening the conditions of your agreement with the Institute."

I'd been well-briefed in the areas in which the Brindesi Institute was rumored to specialize, so Gerlich couldn't trip me up. I didn't put in any disclaimers about the ethics of the Institute's activities, and Gerlich plainly didn't expect me to do so.

At last he leaned back, apparently satisfied with my answers. He took off his reading glasses and replaced them in his top pocket. I smiled politely. "Now, if I may ask a question or two of you, Dr. Gerlich?"

"Concerning the project?"

I nodded. "I have only the broadest understanding of what it might entail, and—"

"Everything's on a need-to-know basis. You will learn only what is required to accomplish your particular task at the time. I'm sure it will become clearer to you as we go along."

He did a visual sweep of the now almost empty room, then pushed his chair back and stood. "Tomorrow afternoon, he said, "two o'clock sharp. I'll meet you at the entrance to the maximum security unit."

Without a word of farewell, he turned and hurried across the room. I looked thoughtfully after him. If Graeme Thorwell was a creep underneath his good looks, I sensed Harry Gerlich was several measures worse. He was poisonously evil.

❧

The rest of the day passed in a haze of fatigue, caused not only because I'd had little sleep, but also because I'd never before been in an undercover role where I had to concentrate quite so hard almost all the time. Playing a therapist was so foreign to me that I was on guard every moment in case I made a slip. And knowing they were recorded, I was constantly being tested by therapy sessions. All in all, it was a high anxiety day.

I did have one unexpected victory. In the afternoon I had a session with a young woman named Holly Taylor, who'd been admitted for treatment of bulimia. I chatted with her for a few minutes, then, following Dr. Jeffrey's instructions, and remembering his practice session with me as patient, I began to speak in a mannered style that presented Holly Taylor with a consistent aural pattern that was not only monotonous, but hypnotic. I went through the procedures for putting Holly into a light trance. And it worked.

I had a ridiculous impulse to dash out and find someone so I could boast, "I've hypnotized someone."

I had less success with Nat Scott, who was in a truculent mood, and spent a good deal of our session staring sulkily at the floor. Mindful of Peter's instructions, I didn't fill the silence, but sat placidly waiting for Nat to speak. I thought longingly of the delights of a good night's sleep and had almost dozed off when Gretchen came to collect my patient.

"In a bit of a grumpy mood, Nat?" she said, flashing a brilliant smile.

"Do you ever get grumpy?" I inquired.

Gretchen looked startled, as though I'd asked if she indulged in something questionable. She considered my question, then said, "I always say, smile and the world smiles with you. Cry and you cry alone."

"Original," I said. "And such good advice."

My ironic tone didn't penetrate her cheery veneer. "I think so," said Gretchen. With a smile.

After Harry Gerlich's inquisition at breakfast, my thoughts had turned to what I might find when I joined the Sanctuary Project. Of course I hadn't brought Estelle Decker's textbook, *The Malleable Brain* with me, but I'd studied the contents as if cramming for an important exam, which in some sense I suppose I had been. It seemed pass-or-fail time was rapidly approaching.

To brainwash a person into becoming a human bomb required someone who was susceptible, a person who could be molded into a fanatic. As all new patients entering Easehaven were given batteries of psychological tests, finding likely candidates for brainwashing would not be difficult. These would not be people with strong self-image, but the uncertain and the lost. Followers, not leaders, who could be induced to believe in something greater than themselves.

I mentally reviewed brainwashing techniques. Although they varied in details, they had common aspects. First, cut the subject off from the outer world. Second, impair judgment and increase suggestibility by drugs, psychological manipulation and/or physical and mental fatigue. Third, intensify the state of altered consciousness. Inadequate sleep, restricted diet, and bombarding the subject with intrusively personal questions would help to achieve shock and confusion. Fourth, arouse strong feelings of fear, excitement or anger until the subject's repressed emotions explode and the person breaks down. And finally, reprogram with the desired thoughts and beliefs—in this case the absolute conviction that one was born to be an agent of death.

Hypnotic techniques had their place in this pattern, particularly in the earlier stages. I guessed this is where Dr. Constance Sommers came in. And Lynda Lane specialized in meditation, another adjunct to brainwashing, as it caused alpha brain waves to predominate until brain activity flattened and suggestibility increased.

I hadn't forgotten Harry Gerlich's expertise with extreme low frequency sound. Estelle Decker and I had discussed ELFs, and she had pointed out that such low bass sounds might explain the phenomena of haunted houses. Unheard by the ears, these undetected low frequencies caused people to experience inexplicable sorrow, deep anxiety or irrational fear. How tempting to attribute these bizarre feelings to ghosts or evil spirits. A brainwashing subject would be similarly terrified by feelings that seemingly came out of nowhere.

I yawned through dinner, much to Daphne's amusement. We were sitting at a table with Phoebe, Dr. Lynda Lane, whose face reminded me more than ever of a hound dog's, and Isabella Nelson, the homely nurse with the beautiful voice I'd met at the Wednesday function.

Although I'd been told that staff and patients intermingling in the dining room was encouraged, looking around the room it was interesting to note how rarely this seemed to happen. Patients—I would never get used to calling them guests—split into small groups or sat by themselves. Medical staff did the same.

"You seem awfully tired, Connie," said Daphne, grinning. "I suppose it's jetlag."

"It's not surprising Dr. Sommers is fatigued," said Isabella. "I believe it's a change of six time zones between the States and Australia. The miracle is that Dr. Sommers is functioning at all."

"Please call me Constance," I said automatically.

"I don't believe in jetlag," Lynda Lane announced in a tone that positively dared jetlag to exist. "It may be a platitude, but mind over matter works every time."

"We'd all be out of work if it did," I said.

My comment seemed to amuse everyone but Phoebe, who frowned. "I don't understand."

Lynda Lane said condescendingly, "Constance means that if our guests here at Easehaven could cure themselves, they wouldn't be here in the first place."

"I see." From the look on Phoebe's doll face, she didn't at all appreciate Lynda's tone. She rallied, however, to say to me,

"Constance, you *must* get a good night's sleep. Fenella van Berg arrives tomorrow and I know Graeme has arranged for you to meet her, as you're part of her daughter's ease team."

"Poor Rosemary," said Isabella.

I laughed. "Why poor Rosemary? Is it because she has to suffer me as a therapist?"

Isabella's blush clashed with her reddish, frizzy hair. "I'm so sorry, Constance. I certainly didn't intend to imply that. What I mean is that Rosemary Lloyd's a very unhappy woman."

"And we're here to change that!" Phoebe was glowing with purpose. "We had a small setback last night, but that's just a hiccup on Rosemary's road to recovery."

Lynda Lane gave a contemptuous snort. "I wasn't aware you had a medical degree, Phoebe."

Phoebe's baby blue eyes narrowed, and her rosebud mouth tightened. There was no mistaking the enmity between them. "I don't have a medical degree, Lynda," she said with dignity, "but I do have human compassion and hope on my side. I strongly believe a positive attitude can work wonders."

I bit my lip to stop my smile. Self-important, bossy and inquisitive Phoebe may be, but I found there was almost something endearing about her at that moment.

Then I thought, *What if this is all a facade? What if Daphne is mistaken, or lying to me, and Phoebe Murdoch is the person pulling all the strings?*

"Gretchen Hamilton shares your optimistic worldview," said Lynda Lane with ill-disguised scorn. "A totally unrealistic stance, in my opinion."

Phoebe appeared ready to explode, so it was fortunate that Graeme Thorwell picked that moment to arrive at the table. His smile was a lower voltage than usual. "I'm having a personal word with every staff member," he said, taking a spare chair and sitting down.

He leaned forward, rested his elbows on the table, and said in a confidential tone, "Tomorrow morning Fenella van Berg, whose generosity, as you know, made Easehaven a reality, will be arriving from the States. She'll be staying for a few days to see her daughter and to look at how the clinic is running in general. I cannot emphasize enough how important it is for every person to ensure that Fenella is treated with the respect and admiration she deserves."

"I'm sure, Graeme, we'll all be as obsequious as necessary," said Lynda Lane with a sardonic smile.

Thorwell ignored her comment, continuing with, "If any of you do have occasion to speak with Fenella, it is of particular importance you couch any reference to Rosemary in very positive terms. Understandably, Fenella is very anxious about her daughter's welfare. She should be reassured by constructive, caring comments."

"Graeme," said Daphne lightly, "you can trust us. We'll grovel, flatter, and generally do the right thing. We all know how important Fenella is."

He nodded his handsome head. "Thank you, everyone, for your cooperation."

"Fenella van Berg," said Isabella, "has more money than sense. Her daughter requires her love and attention, not a psychiatric clinic."

This started a discussion about nature versus nurture that I was too tired to join. "I'm off," I said to Daphne. "I've found life quite strenuous lately, so I need an early night."

She walked with me to my room. "Edward tells me you and Harry Gerlich had a long chat this morning," she said.

I groaned. "Is there nothing that gets by blasted Edward Quoint."

"Not much."

"Dr. Gerlich was checking me out to see if I would be worthy to join the Sanctuary Project."

She looked sideways at me. "Really? Did you pass?"

"It seems so."

Daphne looked thoughtful. "I imagine you have some . . . unusual qualifications."

A chill touched me. Was she referring to the Brindesi Institute? If so, she was more deeply involved in Easehaven's criminal activities than I had hoped. I wasn't falling for Daphne, of course, but I had to admit to myself that I was beginning to care a little too much.

"Dr. Gerlich was won over by my charm," I said flippantly. "Qualifications had nothing to do with it."

Daphne grinned. "I don't believe even you, Connie, could charm Harry." She linked an arm with mine. "If you're involved in the Sanctuary Project, there may be times when you and I will be working together. I'd like that."

"What about with Rosemary Lloyd? I'm to become her principal therapist any day now, and you're head of nursing, Daphne. I imagine Rosemary would demand the best. Surely that's you."

She laughed at my sly smile. "I'm afraid I'm not in Rosemary's good books," she said. "She sees me as a rival for Graeme's affections."

"That's ridiculous."

"Not so ridiculous," Daphne said. "Graeme and I were lovers, once."

CHAPTER ELEVEN

Fenella van Berg arrived at ten on Friday morning. Her limousine drew up at the front entrance and Graeme Thorwell himself rushed out to open the car door. I was an interested spectator, because I was, as of today, officially Rosemary's primary therapist, and had been instructed to join the welcoming committee, made up of Thorwell, Phoebe, and myself. Sean hovered nearby, his adolescent face screwed up into puzzled concentration. Perhaps he was wondering who Fenella van Berg was, or maybe he was worried about making a mess of unloading a VIP's luggage. I gave him a reassuring smile, and he blinked back at me.

Yesterday Graeme Thorwell's patron had flown into Sydney in her private jet, spent the night in the largest suite of a luxury hotel, and this morning had flown in a smaller plane to the nearest airport on the Central Coast.

The limousine, appropriately, was a gleaming imported American vehicle with tinted windows. Thorwell stood by the open door like an obedient servant, and after a moment a heavy-built man with a shaved head emerged. He was wearing a black suit, white shirt and red tie. I immediately recognized him from photographs. This was Waldo Jenkinson, Fenella's long-time bodyguard. He looked our little group over to make sure no one presented an immediate threat, turned slowly to scan 360 degrees, then bent down to report to the occupants of the limo.

Fenella van Berg appeared, her short, squat figure arrayed in a tight, deep orange jumpsuit, guaranteed to clash with Phoebe's pink uniform. Following her was a harried looking woman clutching a briefcase.

"Welcome to Easehaven, Fenella," Thorwell said. "I hope you had a good trip."

Fenella brushed him aside and without speaking, hustled into the building on her thick legs, Jenkinson striding ahead to check no assassin was lurking in the entrance area. The assistant hastened after them, briefcase in hand. Sean, impelled by a glare from Thorwell, moved to assist the chauffeur with unloading the luggage. Satisfied everything was in order, Thorwell hurried after Fenella and party. The rest of the welcoming committee, consisting of Phoebe and me, followed.

Fenella halted in the reception area. Jenkinson looked around suspiciously, probably hoping some threat would materialize to relieve the boredom of his day. I tried to see the outline of a shoulder holster under the excellent cut of his jacket. I was guessing he'd be carrying a concealed weapon, even though Australian law prohibited the possession of handguns, apart from law enforcement officers. There were always some exceptions, and I had no doubt Fenella van Berg's money and influence ensured her bodyguard special dispensation.

Fenella gestured in her assistant's direction. "This is Kym's replacement, Andrea Sullivan," she said to Thorwell. Andrea, a tall thin woman with a hangdog expression, ducked her head apologetically. I had a feeling she wasn't going to last long in the position.

Phoebe, whom I'd expected to take a major role in greeting Fenella, stood silent, her lips pursed, her hands linked in front of her rounded stomach.

We formed a procession to make our way to the luxury apartment kept for executive guests. It was situated next to Thorwell's apartment, and I imagined the rooms would be even more luxurious.

Fenella led at a sparkling pace, with Jenkinson on one side and Graeme Thorwell hurrying along on the other. Next came the assistant, head bent as though she expected something to rise up out of the floor and trip her up. Phoebe and I brought up the rear.

I was interested to get a feel for the relationship between Thorwell and Fenella. So far it seemed serf and aristocrat, with Thorwell playing a particularly subservient role.

When we reached the apartment, Thorwell flung open the door and gestured grandly for Fenella to enter. Jenkinson went first, of course, to inspect for hazards. When he waved the all clear, we all crowded into the formal lounge room. Fenella looked around, giving a grunt of approval at the extravagant arrangements of flowers and the crystal bowl overflowing with exotic fruit.

Fenella van Berg's photographs didn't do her justice. In person she had a brooding quality. Her hooded eyes were those of a raptor, her mouth ready to snap off heads. She had a chunky, dense body, not fat, but solid.

After dispatching Jenkinson to inspect the rest of the apartment, she turned to Phoebe. "See what's happened to my baggage, will you? And have you made sure the chef has been informed of my special food requirements?"

"The chef has been informed, Ms. van Berg, but I'll double check." She practically backed out of the room, and I suddenly realized Phoebe was totally intimidated by this woman.

Apart from the anxious-to-please Thorwell, another person who seemed overwhelmed was the personal assistant, Andrea, who had retreated to a corner of the room and looked as if she would be happy to fade into the wallpaper.

Graeme Thorwell made a big display of introducing me to Fenella. She didn't offer to shake hands. "Constance Sommers?" she said. "Yes, Kym mentioned you."

"Constance will be Rosemary's primary therapist," said Thorwell, hovering nervously. "I've spoken to you about the problems of trans-ference with Rosemary—"

She cut him off with a chopping gesture. "Don't go over it again, Graeme. You know I approve. Under the circumstances you could hardly continue to be Rosemary's doctor." Looking at his expression, I wondered what these circumstances might be. He was not a happy man.

Now she knew my role in her daughter's life, Fenella's attention focused on me. She gave me a head-to-toe inspection, then said, "Can you help her?"

"I can."

A smile broke on her thin-lipped mouth. "Excellent. I like your attitude."

Thorwell looked momentarily relieved, then his apprehensive expression returned as he said, "Fenella, I didn't think it worthwhile contacting you, knowing you were coming here today, but Rosemary did have a little problem last night."

"What sort of problem?"

"She became upset. Cut herself. Just a few minor scratches."

Impatience swept over Fenella's face. "Give me the facts, not your interpretation of them."

"It was a quasi-suicide attempt. Not serious at all. As I said, merely token cuts to her wrists. Rosemary's *much* better this morn-ing. She's lightly sedated, but you'll be able to see her immediately, if you wish."

"Of course I wish!" Fenella swung around, fixing me with a pierc-ing stare. "And what do you think of this?"

As I hadn't been expected to meet Fenella van Berg, ASIO's preparation had not included an in-depth psychological profile. Without this guidance, I was just guessing this was a woman who would like people who stood up to her. If I were wrong, it would be a serious miscalculation. I said, "I believe Rosemary's overwhelmed by you."

Thorwell looked stricken. "Fenella, I—"

She waved him to silence. "Go on," she said to me.

"It isn't rocket science," I said. "You're powerful, strong, directed. Everything Rosemary admires. She's afraid she can't live up to the standards you've set."

A glimmer of humor showed on her heavy features. "Someone who has the sense to be direct. How pleasant, after all the sycophantic fools who surround me."

I didn't flatter myself that Fenella regarded me with any esteem. Rather, I was a means to an end.

"What treatment protocols do you intend to take with my daughter?"

Thorwell broke in with, "Constance has used hypnotherapy with excellent results."

"Hypnotherapy?" she said. "You've had successes with patients like Rosemary?"

"Yes."

"I'll observe a session."

The last thing I wanted was this woman looking over my shoulder. I said, "I'm afraid your presence would unsettle your daughter."

"I won't be in the room with you. I'll use the excellent surveillance system Graeme insisted on installing."

Prudent acquiescence was indicated. I said, "I'll advise you as soon as a session with Rosemary is scheduled."

This matter settled, she turned to Thorwell. "Graeme, I'm not at all happy you failed to contact me immediately about Rosemary. What else are you keeping from me?"

"Nothing at all. I—"

"Nothing? So when Rafe pushed his way in to see my daughter, in your estimation this was not important?"

"How did you—"

"My ex-husband had the astonishing temerity to call me directly, complaining you'd tried to stop him from seeing Rosemary."

Apparently not wishing to be interrupted in mid-sentence again, Thorwell remained silent.

"Is it a coincidence Rosemary cuts herself after seeing her father? Well?" She didn't stop for an answer. "What type of security are you providing? If Rafe can force his way in here, then anybody can. You told me explicitly, Graeme, that Rosemary did not need a personal bodyguard. You guaranteed she'd be safe here at Easehaven."

"She *is* safe here."

"We'll discuss it later." Her gaze settled on Andrea Sullivan. "Andrea, what are you doing?"

"Ah . . . nothing, Fenella."

Fenella's jaw jutted pugnaciously. "Precisely. You know I have important business calls to make, and need the appropriate papers. Where are they?"

"I have them here."

Palpably relieved to have a chance to get away, Thorwell said, "We'll leave you, then, Fenella. I'll see you at lunch. Would you like it served on the patio?"

She flapped her hand impatiently. "I'll decide later, but before lunch I must see Rosemary."

"Of course, of course. Call me as soon as you're free."

Could Thorwell get any more unctuous? Sure, he was spectacularly good-looking, but what was it about this weak man that Daphne had found appealing enough to take him as a lover? I found myself feeling a little sorry for him. His future career appeared to be dependent on Fenella's goodwill, a woman who struck me as the type to squash Thorwell like an insect if the fancy took her.

Outside in the hallway I said to him, "Ms. van Berg has quite a presence."

"She does." He let his breath out in a long sigh. "It's Rosemary I'm worried about. It must be clear to you she's extremely attached to me."

"You mentioned transference before. It's common between psychiatrist and patient."

I said this airily, as if I actually understood the term. I knew it was something to do with strong emotions experienced in childhood for a person, that were transferred in adulthood to someone who hadn't caused them in the first place. I supposed in Rosemary's case it would be her original love and yearning for acceptance from a parent or other adult figure.

Fortunately Thorwell didn't give me a quick quiz on the subject, but only said glumly, "I'm afraid Fenella mistakes Rosemary's attachment for something much more."

I put on the most sympathetic expression I could manage. "That must be difficult for you."

"You have no idea."

I was five minutes early for my appointment with Dr. Harry Gerlich. He was, as I expected, punctual. At two o'clock sharp he appeared, malevolence personified. I had to admit that here, I was doing a bit of transference myself. For some reason Gerlich reminded me of the bogey men of my early childhood, loathsome creatures that lay in wait between clothes hanging in wardrobes or skulked under beds ready to grab a dangling hand or foot.

Entry into the secure area was by electronic keycard used simultaneously with a code punched into a numeric keypad. Obviously borrowing housekeeping's master card wouldn't get me in here.

We entered a long corridor, lined with steel doors. Several had cards with the names of patients indicated. Each door had a sliding metal shutter, so patients in the rooms could be observed by medical staff. It was almost unnervingly silent in the corridor, so our footsteps rang loudly as we walked toward a second security door. Before we reached it I saw Madison Petrie's name. I wished I could comfort her with the news I was close by outside her room, and that one way or another she would be rescued soon.

The Sanctuary Project was also accessed using the keycard and a numeric keypad. At the first door Gerlich had made no effort to hide the numbers he was punching in, so I'd memorized them. This second door used the same keycard, but the combination had to be different, as this time he stood so his body hid the numbers he was selecting.

Here were the same metal doors, each with a little eye-height shutter, to allow someone outside to spy on the confined person. No names appeared anywhere, but each door was numbered. The corridor ended in a comfortable sitting room with a view of the gardens through wide glass windows. He gestured for me to sit, taking a chair opposite mine.

"What we are about to discuss is entirely confidential," he said. "You'll be required to sign a binding agreement to that end. Nothing about the Sanctuary Project procedures, or the identity of the subjects can be mentioned to anyone at any time. Indeed, even with the subjects themselves, the project must not be discussed."

"I quite understand."

Gerlich gave a quick nod, then asked, "You use sound and light in conjunction with hypnosis?"

"I've utilized both frequently. Music can be used to encourage repetitive bodily movements leading to altered states of consciousness. Combined with lighting set to pulse rhythmically, a trance state can be induced, even if the subject attempts to resist." I sounded so convincing I almost pictured myself using these techniques.

Gerlich' sallow face was lit with enthusiasm. "This is excellent, Dr. Sommers. I believe you will find our research project here most rewarding."

"What exactly *is* the research project?"

"We have covert government funding from the intelligence agencies to compare the depth and quality of altered states of consciousness as induced by various means, including meditation, certain drugs, hypnosis and the conversion techniques utilized by various religious organizations. I must emphasize that all subjects are informed volunteers who have willingly signed the requisite releases."

I knew the first of these statements was untrue. The Australian intelligence agencies had not commissioned this project. As for the subjects being informed volunteers, I could not imagine any normal individual would freely submit to a program designed to turn them into directed murderers, so presumably they were deceived about the true purpose of the project, or were too mentally or emotionally disturbed to make a reasoned judgment.

Gerlich tried a pleasant smile, but it curdled on his lips. "Naturally we're not expecting you to perform these extra duties without additional remuneration. I think you'll find us very generous."

"If I may ask, Dr. Gerlich, who is 'we'? All the Easehaven medical staff?"

"Selected people only," he said briskly. Unfolding his body awkwardly from his chair, he said, "Come with me."

We halted in the corridor next to Room Five. Sliding the metal shutter back, he gestured for me to look in. "Verity Young is her name," he said in a sibilant whisper. "Twenty-one, in good health. She's the most promising of three volunteers we have in the unit at the moment."

The walls, ceiling and floor of the rectangular room were flat white. There was no window. Light came from a panel set into the ceiling. The only furniture was a bunk bed suspended from the wall and a plain white chair. A white screen that didn't reach the floor gave some privacy when using the compact bathroom. The whole purpose of the room was to provide the minimum of sensory input.

Verity Young wore a shapeless white shift. She was sitting on the chair, bare feet flat on the floor, hands relaxed on her lap. Her eyes were closed. She had delicate bones and pale skin, as if it had been a long time since she'd seen sunlight. Her light brown hair was loose on her shoulders.

Sliding the shutter closed, Gerlich said, "Lynda Lane has done some exceptional work with Verity regarding meditation techniques. Your work in conjunction with Lynda will be on another subject, Malcolm Ayres. Your aim will be the rapid establishment of a continuous trance state."

Malcolm Ayres? I hadn't heard the name before, but medical privacy provisions had meant ASIO's patient lists had some gaps.

I said, "If I may use a popular term, Dr. Gerlich, what you're describing veers close to brainwashing."

He wasn't the slightest fazed by this. "It does," he agreed blandly. "Verity Young is a patriot who has put herself forward to further research into techniques used by the enemies of democracy."

I could not have made this outrageous statement with a straight face, but Gerlich had no problem at all.

"Surely," I said, "there's a danger that Verity's emotional and mental balance will be permanently affected."

He lifted his narrow shoulders. "A slight chance perhaps," he said dismissively.

We began to walk back the way we'd come. Apparently my visit was over. "We'll go to the office now, and have you sign the required confidentiality agreement," he said. "You'll have your first session with Malcolm tomorrow at nine. All necessary sound and lighting equipment is available, but if you require anything additional, arrangements will be made to provide it as quickly as possible."

"Thank you, but I prefer in my initial contact with a patient to use simple hypnosis to accurately assess the suggestibility of the subject."

"As you wish, Constance." My surprise at the use of my first name showed, because he added, "As we'll be working closely together, I feel it appropriate to be on friendlier terms. You must call me Harry."

When we were outside the entrance door to the area, I said, "Why is it called the Sanctuary Project?"

Without even a trace of irony, Gerlich said, "Because it's a safe haven. The pressures and demands of the world do not intrude here."

I was grabbing a quick cup of coffee before another session with Nat Scott when Phoebe came rushing into the staff sitting room. "Have you seen Dr. Thorwell! I must find him immediately."

"What's up?"

"For this to happen when Fenella van Berg is here! I've called his number, but he's not answering." She flapped her hands helplessly and dashed out of the room. I was curious enough to forgo my coffee and follow her.

In the reception area Edward Quoint was keeping a man under wary observation—a thin, jittery guy who had his hands jammed in his pockets and was pacing up and down. The CIA's Joe Ibbotson.

Phoebe hurried up to him. "Mr. Petrie, I've paged Dr. Thorwell. I'm sure he'll be with you any moment now."

Ibbotson's narrow face was clenched in a fierce scowl. "Now see here," he bleated in his thin voice, "I've flown in from the States expressly to see my sister. I know Madison's somewhere in the clinic, and I suspect you're holding her against her will. Take me to her immediately."

"Mr. Petrie, please calm down." Phoebe tried a placatory smile. "I realize you're upset, but—"

"Who are you? A doctor?" he snapped, looking past her to me.

Obviously relieved to find someone else to take the heat, Phoebe seized my arm and propelled me forward. "Dr. Sommers, this is Mr. Petrie. His sister, Madison, is at present a guest in Easehaven's secure unit. I've been trying to find Dr. Thorwell to explain to Mr. Petrie why he cannot see her at the moment."

"Mr. Petrie," I said soothingly. "Let's sit down and have a chat about the situation."

"I don't want to sit down. I want to see my sister." He glared at Quoint. "And no guy in a pink uniform's going to stop me."

I said to Phoebe, "Dr. Thorwell was intending to have lunch with Ms. van Berg on the patio, I believe."

Chagrin momentarily swamped her concern over the unannounced arrival of this outraged relative. "I wasn't told about lunch!"

"To hell with the lunch," snarled Madison's supposed brother. "Just get the motherfucker here. I'll give you ten minutes to produce this Thorwell guy. Then I'm calling the cops."

With both hands Phoebe made an ineffectual damping gesture. "Please, Mr. Petrie, keep your voice down."

Ibbotson was throwing heart and soul into his act. He actually managed to make his face red as he yelled, "Get him! Now!"

I hid a smile as a flustered Phoebe scuttled off. Edward Quoint raised his eyebrows in an unspoken question. Reading this as should he go or stick around, I said, "You can go, Edward. I'll keep Mr. Petrie company until Dr. Thorwell arrives."

Quoint hesitated, obviously waiting to see if the American had calmed down. Ibbotson practically tap-danced his way over to a lounge chair and subsided into it.

"Sorry for the commotion," he said, jiggling one knee in an irritating rhythm, "but we're all terribly concerned about Madison. We've called numerous times from Ohio and been fobbed off every time. It's very frustrating, and worrying, you understand."

Reassured there would not be mayhem in the reception area, at least not at the moment, Edward Quoint nodded to me and left. Now that silence had fallen, the barely audible, almost subliminal sound of orchestral music could be heard.

Ibbotson cocked his head. "Not much of a sound system," he said. "What do you think of it?"

He was querying if we could be overheard by electronic means. "I don't like music played so softly," I replied, shaking my head. That negative gesture told him not to say anything incriminating.

"Have you seen Madison?" he asked.

"She's not my patient."

"Do you know if she's all right?"

"I'm afraid I can't comment."

He cracked his knuckles fretfully. "If we just knew how she was." He fixed me with a look. "Her best friend, Zena, is frantic. To talk with Madison on the phone would be a great relief."

He was giving me a message to ring Zena urgently. I was working out how to frame a question to get some idea of what it was Zena had to tell me, when Graeme Thorwell, Phoebe in tow, materialized.

"Mr. Petrie," he said smoothly, extending his hand. "I'm Dr. Thorwell."

Ibbotson bounced to his feet. "My sister, Madison, is being held here. I've come to take her home with me."

"I'm afraid that isn't possible, at least not today."

"And why would that be?" Ibbotson asked, with dangerous calm.

"Your sister voluntarily admitted herself to Easehaven because of a bipolar disorder. Unfortunately, a few days later she experienced a severe psychotic episode. For her own safety, she was placed in isolation, carefully evaluated, and then treated with a regimen of drugs to alleviate her symptoms. It would be unsafe to remove her too abruptly from her medications."

"What time frame are we talking about here?"

Thorwell flashed his killer smile. "You'll be pleased to know you can definitely see Madison tomorrow. In the meantime I'll evaluate her progress. It may be possible to release her within the next few days."

"That's not good enough! She's leaving with me now."

"I'm sorry," said Thorwell with the affronted dignity of one whose professional judgment has been questioned, "but the welfare of my patient comes first. It is my considered opinion that to remove her from her medications today, without slowly reducing the dosage, could have serious repercussions."

Ibbotson glared at him. "I want another opinion."

"Another opinion?" Thorwell obviously hadn't anticipated this request. He recovered to say persuasively, "Mr. Petrie, in this geographical area there's no reputable psychiatrist practicing outside Easehaven. It will take some time to get the second opinion you're asking for."

"This doctor here . . ." Ibbotson turned to me. "What's your name? Sommers, is it?" I nodded. Ibbotson went on to Thorwell, "I'll accept a second opinion from Dr. Sommers. She's already told me Madison isn't her patient, so I presume she can give an unbiased evaluation of my sister's condition."

Barely hiding his relief, Thorwell said, "This would be an excellent solution to the problem. Dr. Sommers will see Madison this afternoon. Then tomorrow we'll see what the situation is."

Ibbotson shuffled his feet, checked the knot of his tie. "Tomorrow, then. I'll be back at ten, on the dot." He put up a threatening fist. "And Thorwell? Believe me when I say if this doesn't pan out, I'll bring the cops in. And that's not all. If any harm's been done to Madison, I'll sue you and your clinic. I'll make it my business to get every last red cent you possess."

Thorwell looked stunned, as well he might. I hadn't thought Ibbotson with his high voice could sound quite so intimidating, but he was absolutely convincing in the role of outraged brother.

"I'll see you out, Mr. Petrie," said Phoebe, unconsciously wringing her hands. It was plain she wanted him off the premises as quickly as possible, and certainly before Fenella could get wind of the situation.

Thorwell and I watched them walk away, Phoebe practically skipping to keep up with Ibbotson long-legged stride. "The long and the short," I remarked, referring to the disparity in their heights.

"What?" Thorwell was clearly distracted.

"Nothing," I said. "Now, about Madison Petrie. Is there a problem?"

Thorwell's chiseled features showed considerable turmoil. "Harry will not be pleased," he said.

Two hours later I got my first glimpse of Madison Petrie. She was curled up, deeply asleep, on a hospital bed. Her skin tone was good, and she was breathing evenly.

Like Verity's all-white cell, this one had white walls and ceiling, but the floor was a hard, gray surface and there was a window letting in natural light.

Thorwell handed me her medical chart from the bottom of the bed. "As you see, her vital signs are excellent."

"Hmmm," I said.

Harry Gerlich, obviously furious, whispered something to Thorwell. I continued to study the chart, while listening hard. Helped by the silence in the room, I caught some words.

" . . . strict timetable . . . we're committed . . . too valuable to discontinue . . . buy the brother off?"

Gerlich's final words caused Thorwell to shake his head violently. "It'll never work, Harry. I had a hell of a time convincing Petrie to come back tomorrow. He was talking about getting the police involved. And of suing me. If Fenella learns about this she—"

"Fenella won't." He turned his black gaze on me. "Unless someone tells her."

"It won't be me telling anyone anything," I said, thinking how I couldn't wait to get Zena on the line. I added helpfully, "I'd be more worried about Edward Quoint spreading the story."

"Oh, *shit*!" Thorwell's face seemed to have gone several shades paler. "How would he know anything about it?"

"Quoint was babysitting Petrie in the reception area while Phoebe tried to locate you."

"Oh, shit," he said again.

Gerlich jerked his head in the direction of the door. "Find him. Shut him up."

When Thorwell had left, Gerlich said to me, "As I mentioned earlier, you'll be well paid for your additional duties, but Petrie's appearance has added an unforeseen complication. In order for our vital work to go forward, this whole affair must be handled discreetly, so you may be required to . . . dissemble when speaking with Mr. Petrie."

"You'll be releasing his sister?"

"I see no alternative," he ground out, glaring at the sleeping woman as though she had deliberately caused him angst. "It will mean we have to recruit a new subject within the next few days. We're working on a strict timetable here, and must have results on schedule."

"I see," I said, drawing out the last word.

He looked at me sharply. "I'll tell you exactly what to say to Petrie. I'm relying on you to smooth things over. He must have no inkling of the Sanctuary Project."

"What about her?" I said, pointing at Madison's unconscious body. "She knows about it."

I found his faint smile infinitely creepy. "I believe I can guarantee selective amnesia. She'll remember very little about her stay at Easehaven." He paused, then said, "Because of these extra duties, I propose to double your present salary package. Other benefits we can discuss later. Do we understand each other, Constance?"

"Yes, Harry, we understand each other very well."

CHAPTER TWELVE

I had no more scheduled patient sessions that afternoon, so I grabbed my cell phone and binoculars, intending to go for a stroll along the headland and call Zena. I was reasonably confident no electronic scanners were being used at Easehaven, so all I needed was a vantage point from which I could make sure no one was close enough to hear my end of the conversation.

Before I got outside, however, I was stopped by Phoebe. "Fenella van Berg wants to see you immediately. She's with Rosemary."

"Can't it wait?"

Phoebe looked absolutely scandalized. "Ask Fenella to *wait*? I don't think so!"

"What if I have something very important to do?"

"Nothing can be more important," said Phoebe with conviction.

"Oh, all right," I said with bad grace.

"I'll take you there."

"Phoebe, I know the way."

"I assured Ms. van Berg I'd find you and bring you to her."

I nodded wearily. It seemed Phoebe's petty tyranny had been superseded by Fenella's genuine despotism.

Rosemary Lloyd looked very much as she had when we'd begun our first one-to-one conversation, that is, sulky, surly and unlikely to please. She was sitting on the dainty little sofa, her legs crossed so one foot was free to pump up and down.

She didn't deign to say hello, but did unbend enough to acknowledge me with a brief nod.

Her mother, still resplendent in the orange jumpsuit, was standing in front of her, arms folded. "Good afternoon, Dr. Sommers."

I put my phone and binoculars down on the nearest table. "Good afternoon, Ms. van Berg."

Fenella turned her attention to her daughter. "Dr. Sommers will be your therapist, Rosemary. I'm expecting you to cooperate fully with her."

Good luck, I thought.

"I only want Graeme," said Rosemary, shooting out her lower lip. I yearned to take a mirror, shove it in her face, and say, *Just take a good, hard look at yourself, you big baby.*

Fenella was no more impressed by Rosemary's reaction than I was. "Don't behave like a spoilt child," she snapped. "We can't always have what we want in life."

Rosemary glowered at her. "Oh, really, Mom? That's *so* convincing, coming from you. Every time you want something, you get it. *I* don't."

It seemed appropriate for a doctor to say something soothing at this point, so I put on my therapist's neutral voice and said, "Rosemary, if you could have anything in the world, what would it be?"

"Not you as my therapist, that's for sure."

Fenella lost her temper, a fearsome sight. She seemed to grow larger, and, if possible, more formidable. She unfolded her arms, clenched her fists, and shoved her face so close to Rosemary's their noses almost touched.

"Rosemary, from the moment you were born I made sure you had the best of everything. And how do you repay me? You've never completed a course of study, you've never worked at a job, you've never achieved anything I wanted for you."

It was time for Rosemary to fold *her* arms. She stared fixedly at the end of her nervously kicking foot and said, "I'm sorry to be such a complete disappointment."

"What is it that would make you happy?" I asked.

Rosemary ignored me, giving the answer to her mother. "I want Graeme. And he likes me, more than likes me. He really does."

"Then Graeme can't be your therapist," Fenella declared.

"Why not?"

"Because he can't have a relationship with you if you're his patient."

Suddenly fired with energy, Rosemary stared at her mother. "Are you saying what I think you're saying?"

"Agree to a course of therapy with Dr. Sommers. When she says she's satisfied with your progress, you can announce your engagement to Graeme Thorwell, but not a moment before."

I couldn't help asking, "Does Graeme Thorwell know about his pending engagement?"

"It won't be a total surprise to him."

Rosemary leapt up, flung her arms around her mother, and cried as she hugged her, "Oh, this is really, really great, Mom! Really great!"

The headland at late afternoon was very pleasant. In case someone was watching from the house, I wandered along, stopping often to look through my binoculars at the birds wheeling above me. Seagulls squawked, a light breeze rustled the foliage, and the rhythmic beat of the sea played counterpoint. A storm had been forecast for the evening, but so far there was no sign of it.

Zena answered after ten rings. "It's Connie," I announced.

"As an added precaution," said Zena, "the transmission from my end is scrambled, but you're not fully protected, so be careful what you say."

I wondered why the transmission from ASIO had been electronically scrambled. It was a dead giveaway if someone was scanning my call, because it implied the person at the other end of the line had something to hide.

"I'm sitting on a big rock near the end of the headland," I said conversationally. "It's a beautiful day."

The boulder on which I was perched was near the edge, so I could hear the pounding waves even more clearly than before. The cliff fell away sheer, so no one could climb up to hear what I was saying. The vegetation in this exposed area was low and sparse, not offering shelter to an eavesdropper. Even so, I had to constantly keep in mind someone could be listening.

"We're scrambling this because I need to give you specific information no one must know you have," Zena said.

"Such as?"

"Norah Bradley is dead."

"Really? Tell me about it."

"Her body was buried in a shallow grave in thick bushland south of Sydney. A surveying party found her entirely by chance. Animals had partly uncovered the remains and someone literally tripped over an exposed arm."

"That's very interesting."

"It is," said Zena. "Body's badly decomposed. Identity established by dental records. Post mortem shows no obvious injuries. Death occurred two to three weeks ago. Full forensic examination of the site, testing of tissues, blood, etcetera hasn't been completed. Her identity's being kept quiet for the moment. No one's been advised, not even next of kin." She paused, then said, "And in case you were speculating who might have done this, no suspects at this time, but one tantalizing bit of information from a security camera raises the possibility Norah Bradley was in the company of a woman on the Campbelltown railway station somewhere around the time she was killed."

Campbelltown was south of Sydney. "Friend, perhaps?"

"No idea who the second person was," said Zena. "Very blurry image, but seemed to be female. We're not even a hundred percent positive it was Norah Bradley."

I suddenly thought of Phoebe and Ibbotson walking away from me and Thorwell. "And the long and the short of it is?"

Zena laughed. "Height? Norah Bradley was a couple of centimeters shorter than you. Unfortunately the surveillance camera shows both of them sitting on a railway station bench, which makes estimation of the person's height difficult. Educated guess? About the same as Norah, give or take a bit."

Being Zena, once the available information was given, she immediately switched to the next topic. "Joe Ibbotson's anxious for feedback. What's happening with Madison Petrie?"

"I'm sure he'll be pleased."

"They're releasing her?"

"Absolutely." I added as a caveat, "Perhaps not quite the same as before."

"How much damage? Her memory?"

"Probably." To be reassuring, I added, "Pretty sure it'll be okay in the end."

"We'll have a psychiatrist standing by."

I wanted to tell Zena about Malcolm Ayres, the new subject for the program, but could think of no way to mention a name without tipping off a listener—if there was one—that I was openly discussing confidential information.

However, if someone were listening to my end of the conversation, there'd be nothing suspicious about Connie Sommers gossiping with a friend, so I said, "It's so interesting working at Easehaven. I've got quite friendly with Daphne Webster, head of nursing."

"And how friendly would that be?" Zena asked, amused.

"I'm sure that's a rhetorical question, so I'll ignore it," I said. "Anyway, Daphne was telling me that she and Graeme Thorwell were lovers once."

"Lovers?" said Zena, plainly intrigued. "There's been no suggestion of that before. Are you sure she isn't spinning a story?"

"I believe she meant it."

"We'll look into it. I've two more things for you. First, Patsy Kimble, who blew herself up at the peace rally in London, didn't activate the device herself. There was a trigger mechanism similar to the one Josetta Wilson used, but a TV news crew had Patsy Kimble on screen at the key moment, and both her hands were in view. The backup in the audience detonated the charge."

"Oh, dear, I do so like solitude, and there's someone coming my way," I said. A slim, athletic figure was walking rapidly toward me.

"Then I'll be brief," said Zena. "We've isolated a possible client for Graeme Thorwell's business venture into contract killing."

"Not only his," I said, waving to Daphne, who was still out of earshot.

"Harry Gerlich?"

"Yes."

"Is he top dog?"

"I think so, yes. Sorry, I'll have to go in a minute."

"Okay, here's a name of a possible new client. We've had surveillance on all Thorwell's channels of communication. He used a cell phone purchased for a dummy company to contact Stafford Earle, and later had a secret meeting with him. Repeat, Stafford Earle. You know him?"

"I do. Goodbye, so nice to talk with you."

As I flipped the phone closed, Daphne halted in front of me. "Hi. Been looking for you everywhere."

"I've been out here enjoying the last of the day."

127

She joined me on the boulder, which had room enough for two to sit comfortably side by side. "You don't mind about Graeme, do you?"

"I'm sorry . . . ?"

"Graeme and me. I'd hate it if it made a difference. What I mean is, I really like you, Connie."

I said with perfect truth, "I like you, too."

"So it's okay?"

"Of course."

We both contemplated the view for a few moments, then I said, "About you and Graeme . . ."

"Hah! I knew it was worrying you."

"I'm not worried, I just . . . Okay, to be truthful, it did get to me a bit. Are you still lovers?"

"God, no!" Daphne's reaction was immediate, and convincing. "Please believe me, we're just good friends." She added, after a pause, "Graeme's too weak for me, too easy to push around. It would never work in the long run."

"Harry Gerlich certainly pushes him around."

Daphne laughed. "Doesn't he! I've urged Graeme to stand up to Harry, but he folds every time."

"Would he fold every time for Fenella?"

I expected her to freely agree he would. When she didn't answer, I turned my head to find her frowning at me. "Is she up to something?" Her tone was intense.

"What makes you think she is?"

"Phoebe told me you'd been summoned to a meeting with Fenella."

I raised my eyebrows. "Is absolutely nothing a secret around here?"

My lighthearted comment didn't lessen Daphne's frown. She said, "What does Fenella want?"

"It's what Rosemary wants. She has her heart set on becoming Graeme Thorwell's wife. And her mother pretty well promised she would."

"It can't happen." There was no equivocation in Daphne's voice.

"Why not? Fenella didn't seem to think Graeme would be all that surprised by the news."

"It's impossible," said Daphne, "because Graeme's already married."

Jenkinson, his shaved head gleaming, stopped me on my way to the evening meal. As always, I had a good appetite and was looking forward to some of the excellent food provided by the kitchen.

"Ms. van Berg wants to see you."

This would be the third time today. What was with this woman? "Right now? Couldn't it wait until after dinner?"

The bodyguard's wooden expression didn't change, nor did he say anything. He just loomed over me, waiting for me to acquiesce. Which, naturally, I did.

"Take me to your leader," I said cheerfully.

We walked to Fenella's apartment with him half a step behind me. He was taller and much stronger, but I decided I could take him, provided I had the element of surprise. Snap kick to knee, then fingers driven into throat, I thought. Not, of course, that I had any idea of attacking Fenella van Berg's bodyguard.

"Something funny?" he said as we reached Fenella's door. "You have a Cheshire Cat grin."

"If I'm the Cheshire Cat, I'll disappear," I said.

"Don't try it." He used a plastic keycard to open the door, then stood aside. "In you go," he said.

Fenella was draped in a pale blue lounging outfit and holding a martini glass. "Ah, Dr. Sommers," she said, "thank you for coming."

"Mr. Jenkinson was very persuasive."

Jenkinson smirked, then made himself scarce.

Fenella offered me a drink. I graciously refused. She said, "There was an altercation with a patient's relative this afternoon. What was it about?"

Obviously Thorwell had failed to shut Edward Quoint up, and word had got back to Fenella. I briefly explained the situation, taking the line that it was no big deal.

She listened to me without comment, then said, "Can I be frank, Dr. Sommers?"

"Please."

"When reporting to me, Graeme is inclined to sugarcoat any problems. This is not an efficient management style, as I've pointed out to him many times. As you might imagine, I have a great deal of money tied up in Easehaven, not to mention the two other clinics. That means I am always very interested in everything concerning both the financial and medical sides of the business."

She paused, giving me time to wonder where in the hell this was going. Nothing ASIO had turned up had indicated she was aware of the special project being run by Gerlich and Thorwell, so it had to be something else.

"I like your manner with Rosemary," she said. "Too many people are inclined to give into her. You seem to me to be a level-headed, reliable woman."

Praise, indeed! I hid a smile.

"I sense something is going on at Easehaven. I'm asking you to find out what it is, and report back to me. I will make it well worth your while."

"Surely Dr. Thorwell—"

"Graeme will not be forthright. To be brutally frank, I believe he's mixed up in something and is in over his head. This is not the first time I've had to rescue him from the results of his own misjudgments. Graeme does engender extraordinary allegiance from his staff. The fact that you're new, and therefore unlikely to feel the same way, is an advantage."

"I'm not sure I like the idea of spying on someone," I said virtuously.

Fenella had an answer for that. "Look upon it as your duty to your patient," she said. "Rosemary has her heart set on marrying

Graeme, and as her therapist, you must have her best interests always in mind."

If what Daphne had said to me was true, Graeme Thorwell was already married. I wouldn't put it past Fenella to use her clout to arrange a lightning divorce, but at least for the moment, Thorwell seemed to be unavailable.

"Are you thinking of a long engagement?" I said.

Fenella frowned, clearly thinking this was none of my business. "I fail to see—" she began.

"Because," I said, taking some pleasure in the fact I was interrupting her for a change, "this will have impact on Rosemary's long term treatment."

I was astonished when she said, "I believe I should be guided by you, Dr. Sommers. When you make the professional judgment that Rosemary is well enough to cope, the marriage can go ahead."

It was dark before I had a chance to call Zena again. After dinner I slipped away for an evening stroll, hoping not to run into any other nocturnal wanderer. The promised storm was well on the way and a chill wind was blowing the sound of the rising surf. The moon shone intermittently through scudding clouds and now and then a flash of lightning flickered far out to sea. I kept to the middle of the headland, not wanting to tumble over the cliff in the darkness. Fortunately the pending bad weather had discouraged anyone else from braving the elements, so I didn't have to walk too far before I felt safe to make the call.

"Zena?"

"Connie, so soon?"

"I've some very interesting news."

"I have some for you too, but you go first."

"Okay," I said, "this'll make you blink. When I told Daphne this afternoon I'd been present when Fenella had promised Rosemary that Thorwell would marry her, the news went down like a lead balloon. Daphne said Thorwell was already married."

"We found no record of a prior marriage," said Zena, sounding miffed. "When, where and who?"

"Las Vegas, September last year. Daphne Webster married Graeme Thorwell in one of those sausage machine wedding chapels. Marriage of convenience, I'm assured."

Even though I was supposed to stick to generalities at my end of the conversation, I had to give Zena more details. "Taking a chance, I know, but I have to be more direct, Zena. Thorwell has been siphoning large sums of money away from the clinics for his retirement fund. Retirement from being Fenella's yes man, that is. There's the source of Daphne's millions."

"Why did Thorwell need to marry her?"

It was a question I'd also asked. "Daphne gave two reasons. First, she said she demanded marriage as a safeguard for her interests. She's expecting to be well-paid for her efforts, but as she says, Thorwell's a weak man. If Fenella got wind of the scheme, she'd try to make sure Daphne got nothing. The second reason is that it's an insurance policy for Thorwell, to be called in if Fenella tells him to marry Rosemary, a command he's apparently been dreading for some time."

"And now she's issued the command."

"Things are going to hit the fan around here pretty soon," I said.

Zena said, "I'm asking myself, why did Daphne tell you all this?"

"I think because she looks on me as a friend, someone to confide in." Ridiculously, I felt a pang of guilt because I was deceiving Daphne so completely.

"A fast friendship," said Zena dryly. "It's more than that, isn't it?"

"No comment."

"Be careful. Don't get emotionally involved."

"Not me."

Zena snorted. Unfortunately, she knew me well.

"We have a possible target," she said. "You recall Kenneth Henders was Stafford Earle's business partner. They had a falling out."

Earle & Henders had been a hugely successful investment company. I well remembered the bitter public fight between the partners. Henders had not only negotiated to gain control of the company behind Earle's back, he had also stolen away Earle's glamorous wife. Ultimately the partnership had been dissolved in the courts with Henders gaining the more advantageous settlement. Earle had divorced his wife and then attempted to bring private legal action against Henders. When this failed, Henders had rubbed salt in the wound with a very showy wedding to Earle's ex-wife. He was at present working on a career in politics, and being a natural demagogue, had captured the interest of the media, who followed his exploits with flattering attention.

"Are there opportunities coming up?"

"Too many. Henders has various public appearances, speeches at functions such as a symposium on Pacific Rim business initiatives. You name it, like any would-be politician, he's in it." She went on to give me dates and venues. "It's a nightmare trying to keep tabs on him."

"Have we approached him?"

"Through channels. At the moment he's playing macho, refusing to cancel anything. Call me tomorrow if you can. I'll have info on the Vegas wedding, plus more up-to-date details of Henders' schedule."

Zena was amused by my description of my meeting with Fenella, but sobered immediately when I mentioned Verity Young as my pick for the next killing. "There's also a young man called Malcolm Ayres," I said, "who's the replacement for Madison. There's a hurry to get him ready, because the time frame's two months."

When I flipped the phone shut, I felt as if a lifeline had been cut. If someone at Easehaven had been eavesdropping with a scanner, I was toast.

133

I carefully made my way back to the clinic, buffeted by heavy wind gusts. Inside, I blinked in the bright light, shucked my jacket and made my way to the staff TV lounge where a raucous group was watching the latest reality show. Joyce Parsons, Daphne's deputy head of nursing, was a natural mimic, and had everyone in stitches with her spot-on impersonations of characters on the screen.

I joined in the laughter, thinking there was safety in numbers, but when no one came to carry me away, I decided I was becoming paranoid, smiling to myself that I'd chosen just the right place to do it.

Daphne came off duty, helped herself to coffee, and joined in the hilarity. After a few minutes she caught my eye and gave an almost imperceptible nod in the direction of the door. As I joined her outside the TV lounge a loud crack of thunder overhead shook the building. We went to the nearest window. It was a spectacular electrical storm. Huge drops of rain were falling, wind was howling, the gardens flickered in and out of view as lightning flashed around us. The thunder became an almost continuous roll of deafening noise.

Daphne put her mouth to my ear. "A perfect night to snuggle up in bed," she said.

I could not but agree.

CHAPTER THIRTEEN

Saturday morning began with an early session with Malcolm Ayres, the new subject for Sanctuary's blend of brainwashing and business. Lynda Lane, looking rather like a benevolent grandmother, collected me in the dining room after breakfast. "Harry's told you about Malcolm?" she asked as we entered the Sanctuary Project area.

"Not a word, other than he's the latest volunteer."

Lynda unlocked Door Three and ushered me inside. It was a windowless room, identical to that of Verity Young's. A young man, looking to be in his early twenties, sat listlessly on the edge of his bunk. He wore a white cotton top and matching white pants. His feet were bare. He looked up incuriously as we entered.

Lynda put a kindly hand on his shoulder. "Malcolm has already begun a drug regimen," she said to me. "This should enhance the altered state of consciousness your hypnotherapy achieves." She went over to the door to call down the corridor, "Isabella? We're ready."

Within a few moments Isabella Nelson wheeled in a monitoring machine. "Morning," she said to me.

Ever polite, I responded, "Good morning, Isabella."

"Quite a storm last night."

"It was," I agreed.

There was something different about her. I checked her out: same melodious voice, same shapeless body, same squarish, plain face. It was the hair. Her former reddish, frizzy hair had been tinted brown—a particularly dull, unflattering brown.

I watched her skillfully attach various leads to the unresisting Malcolm, who seemed to me too dazed to be a good hypnotic subject—but then, what did I know?

Lynda Lane took me aside to say, "I'm afraid your session with Malcolm will be a rather brief one, as Graeme's arranged to release Madison Petrie today. Her brother's arriving at ten o'clock to pick her up."

There was a note of disapproval in her voice, and I picked up on that with, "It seems such a waste at this point to release Madison."

Lynda looked a little surprised. "Harry Gerlich's given you all the details?"

"We discussed the situation yesterday."

It was odd, but this simple statement appeared to do more than reassure Lynda, it made me her instant confidante. "It's a great shame. We have a strict timetable to meet, and although Malcolm here is an adequate backup, Madison Petrie's background made her an ideal subject."

I presumed she meant the fact Madison apparently had all her family and friends in another country, too far away for personal visits. "When does he have to be ready?" I asked, indicating the young man, who appeared oblivious to the many wires connected to his head and chest attaching him to gently beeping machines.

"Graeme has the details. I've heard two months, but that's not firm. It could be earlier, it could be later."

"Well, you've covered all the possibilities," I said with a smile.

Lynda Lane didn't return the smile. She said gravely, "Harry Gerlich may not have told you this. We've had failures. So there is a third possibility. Unfortunately, since the program began, we've lost two."

"You mean they died?"

"One suicide, one anaphylaxis."

I knew anaphylaxis was a severe allergic reaction to something swallowed or injected. "Bad luck," I said.

Lynda took my comment at face value. "It was. A very big contract fell through. Our bonuses were affected, of course."

Our bonuses? After every successful suicide-murder, people got bonuses?

"A real shame," I said.

I really was starting to get the hang of this hypnotherapy thing. Working on Malcolm was nerve-wracking, as I knew I was being observed through the fisheye lens of the camera above the door. Once I got into the swing of things, I was able to attain a relatively deep trance state quite easily. It was fascinating to see one of the machines displaying the changes in his brain wave patterns as he slipped deeper into altered consciousness.

I asked him questions—all innocuous—and ran through the series of suggestibility tests Dr. Reynolds had taught me. Somewhere along the line I became aware I was being watched through the peephole in the door, but I still started when Lynda Lane said, "You'll have to bring this session to a close, Constance. Mr. Petrie's arrived early."

My skin prickled when I found Harry Gerlich waiting for me outside the high security section. He thrust a manila folder into my hand. "Make sure Petrie signs the release form. There's also a statement listing medications given to his sister and details of her treatment. If she had in reality had a psychotic episode, the drugs indicated would be prescribed by any competent psychiatrist."

I gestured with the folder. "This is all lies, basically."

137

A nasty little smile twitched his lips. "There are lies, and then there are lies. We tell the ones that are profitable. Very profitable. If you have scruples, tell me."

"Not one scruple," I said. "Where's Madison Petrie now?"

"I worked on her half the night. She's conscious, vital signs good, memory shot to pieces." Gerlich almost rubbed his hands in satisfaction. "Isabella will bring her down in a wheelchair once you've got Petrie to sign the release."

"Okay."

I turned to go, but he put cold fingers on my arm. It was all I could manage not to recoil with repugnance. "I've always found lies are best kept to a minimum. So don't discuss his sister's medical treatment in any detail. Refer Petrie to the written record if he asks questions."

I eased my arm away. "Thanks for the advice."

Joe Ibbotson was practically moon-walking his way around the reception area. "Where is she?" he barked the moment he saw me.

Phoebe fluttered around him, quite a feat for a stout little woman. "Madison will be here directly, Mr. Petrie. Directly. Please sit down."

"I don't want to sit down. I want my sister."

Frankly, I thought he was rather overplaying his role this morning, so I said in a cool tone, "Mr. Petrie, please do take a seat." I handed him the manila folder. "Here is a medical release for you to sign, and details of Madison's stay at Easehaven you may wish to review."

He reluctantly lowered himself into a chair. "You examined Madison?"

"Yes."

"And?"

"She's very tired and a little confused at the moment. I'm confident that by tomorrow you will see considerable improvement."

He signed the release with a flourish and gave it to me. Then he turned his head to glower at Phoebe. "You," he said, pointing, "you're the administrator for this place, aren't you?" Phoebe nodded warily.

"Am I to expect some exorbitant bill from you? Some creative bookkeeping indicating Madison owes the clinic a small fortune? Plus whatever Thorwell cares to demand for his questionable services?"

"Dr. Thorwell's waived all charges, Mr. Petrie."

"Really? Sounds like your boss has something to hide."

Oh, Ibbotson, don't go there, I thought, seeing how he was really getting considerable enjoyment out of terrorizing Phoebe. I wanted him and the CIA plant out of the place before anything could go wrong.

"Your sister's arrived," said Phoebe, clearly relieved.

Isabella Nelson maneuvered the wheelchair bearing Madison to a smooth stop by Ibbotson's chair. "Here we are then," she said to Madison, in that annoying way some nurses use the royal plural. "We're feeling a little tired this morning, aren't we?"

Ibbotson was up and gazing intensely into his supposed sister's face. "Madison?"

"Oh, hi . . ."

Ibbotson, like me, had realized she might be so confused by drugs she'd blurt something out, so he said quickly, "Don't say a word. Save your strength. I'm getting you out of here right now."

He seized the handles of the wheelchair, released the brake, and took off at a fast clip toward the entrance, Isabella hurrying after him. "Excuse me! Excuse me! A member of staff must operate the wheelchair."

As they disappeared out the front door, I turned to Phoebe. "Thank God that's over," I said.

She nodded, her porcelain features wan. "Yes," she said in a heartfelt tone.

For a moment we were silent, sharing the same deep feeling of relief, but for entirely different reasons.

"You'd better report to Graeme," I said. "He'll be anxious to know everything went well."

"Yes, he will."

There was a reason behind my suggestion. Teena wasn't in the office on Saturdays, and I wanted Phoebe out of the way so I could look at staff records.

Thankfully, Teena was methodical, so the material was up-to-date. I'd memorized the password on the first day, but I made sure it hadn't been changed by checking the desk's top drawer where Teena obligingly had it written down.

I was looking for dates where staff had been away from Easehaven. In London, Patsy Kimble hadn't pulled the trigger on the bomb she'd been wearing—it had been detonated by a radio signal. In Sydney, Josetta Wilson had killed Senator O'Neven with a bomb that could also be detonated remotely, although it seemed in that case she had pulled the trigger. There had almost certainly been a backup in the audience to detonate the bomb if she chickened out at the last moment. More than likely the person was someone from the Sanctuary Project.

It took some time, and I was poised to shut down the screen if anyone appeared, but eventually I had the material I needed. Two people had been absent for three days, spanning the date of the suicide bombing: Daphne Webster and Isabella Nelson.

Daphne. I had a vision of last night, thunder and lightning theatrically flashing and booming outside, while we made our own storm in Daphne's bed.

Afterwards, wound around each other in warm comfort as the rain pelted against the window, Daphne had said, "What did Fenella want with you?"

I'd laughed. "Are you spying on me?"

"Phoebe saw you being escorted to Fenella's apartment, presumably for an audience with the woman herself."

I played it safe with, "She's worried about Rosemary."

"*Rosemary*." There was a world of scorn in her voice.

"Not your favorite person?"

"You could say that." She'd moved restlessly, then said, "Did she mention Graeme?"

"Daphne, would you divorce him?" I didn't have confirmation of the marriage yet from Zena, but somehow I was sure it was genuine.

Daphne became very still. "Why are you asking?"

"It's obvious, isn't it? Fenella's determined to have him marry Rosemary, but legally he's not free."

"And it's going to stay that way."

"But, why?"

She'd pulled me to her in a close embrace. "It's to do with money, Connie. I deserve to be repaid for all I've done for Graeme. I can't explain, but trust me when I say Graeme's potential is virtually unlimited. Soon he'll be able to dump Fenella and her bloody daughter."

We'd melted into a long, languorous kiss. "I'm beginning to care for you, Connie," she'd breathed against my lips. "Care a lot."

"Me too."

Another kiss, then Daphne had said, "So what else did Fenella want to know?"

I considered how much to say, then decided to approximate the truth. "Fenella thinks something is going on at Easehaven."

"Like what?"

"She wasn't specific. I get the impression she thinks Graeme's in some sort of trouble."

I could feel Daphne's body tense. "She didn't mention the Sanctuary Project, did she?"

"No. Is she supposed to know anything about it?"

An emphatic, "No!" Then more moderately, she added, "It's treated as part of the maximum security section for seriously disturbed patients."

"I haven't seen you there," I said. "In the Sanctuary area, I mean. You told me before you had something to do with it."

"I'm more on the organizational side." She'd stretched, yawned. "God, I've got to get up early in the morning. I'll have to get some sleep."

Subject closed.

I'd kissed her goodnight, got dressed, and gone back to my own room, realizing what mental gymnastics I'd been engaged in, trying to put Daphne in the best light, no matter how damning the evidence. Reluctantly I had to admit to myself she must have at least some idea of the Sanctuary Project's true purpose, particularly if her concern was the organization of the unit. Even so, I wanted to think if she were involved, it was only peripherally.

My first session with Rosemary as her official therapist was slated for Monday morning, and I wasn't looking forward to it. I spent Sunday doing my laundry and taking a solitary drive along the coast road. When I was sure I wasn't being followed, I stopped at a lookout high above the water to admire the aftermath of the storm. Huge waves rolled in, smashing themselves into foam on a deserted curve of sandy beach. The air was washed clean and there was a sense of spring in the air.

I thought of Verity Young, imprisoned in a white cell, her mind enslaved. Of Malcolm's vacant stare. They were being prepared to join Josetta, Anita and Patsy in death. A warm flush of rage made me tingle. It was going to stop. Whatever it took, Thorwell and Gerlich and every other person associated with the obscenely-named Sanctuary Project would be brought to justice.

When I called Zena she took longer than usual to answer. "Sorry, we've got a committee here trying to establish the most likely venue for the hit on Henders."

"Have you got one?"

"One? We've got about five or six scheduled appearances, not to mention his spontaneous clusters, as he so fetchingly calls them."

By spontaneous clusters, Zena was referring to the way Henders had been using the resources of email and instant messaging to arrange spur-of-the-moment gatherings of people in public places.

The technique had been extraordinarily effective, often creating substantial crowds in a matter of minutes at previously unscheduled locations. Established politicians had been caught flat-footed by this instant-crowd, spur-of-the-moment phenomenon.

Zena went on, "We're actively discouraging any unscheduled gatherings and Henders has promised he'll cooperate. His first scheduled appearance is on Friday afternoon, so we have time to set up extra security."

"He's not willing to cancel?"

"No such luck! Henders won't hear of canceling anything. He's convinced he's invulnerable, but he's also really enjoying the attention from ASIO and the Federal Police."

"Does he have a personal bodyguard?" I asked.

"If you can call him that. He's an ex-bouncer with mush for brains. Simpson, his name is." She added, dryly, "We're not relying on him to be any help in an emergency, rather like his boss."

"You're not a fan of Henders, are you?" I asked.

"The man's a compulsive show-off of the most odious sort."

"I hope that's not a political remark." Officially, ASIO staff were public servants, schooled not to reveal personal political affiliations.

Zena laughed, then said, "Daphne Webster was telling the truth. She is legally married to Graeme Thorwell."

"And Daphne told me last night she wouldn't divorce him, under any circumstances."

"This will dash Rosemary Lloyd's dreams of wedded bliss."

"Too true." I said this lightly, but I was feeling apprehensive about how she'd take the news, which I was sure would leak somehow. Rosemary had attempted suicide before, although how seriously was in question. I was pretending to be a therapist, and if Fenella turned to me for help, what would I do? I couldn't treat Rosemary as a genuine medical professional, and I couldn't blow my cover. I pushed the thought away. I'd worry about it when, and if, it happened.

"You gave me the names of Verity Young and Malcolm Ayres. We've found Malcolm Ayres—he's from some remote town in Western Australia, but there's no record of a Verity Young that fits the age profile. Perhaps she's foreign. Have you heard her speak? Does she have an accent?"

"I've only seen her through a peephole in the door. She was comatose and said nothing. Because Malcolm Ayres has just started the brainwashing program, and they've lost Madison Petrie, I'm sure Verity will be the one they'll use next."

"What's she look like?"

I gave Zena a brief description.

"That could fit countless young women."

Zena was right. Put Verity Young in crowd of people, dressed like anyone else her age, and she'd blend right in. She was a normal, pleasant looking individual with nothing particularly notable about her.

"I've information on the backup in the audience," I said.

"You have a candidate?"

"Two. Isabella Nelson and Daphne Webster. Both were absent from Easehaven for a time corresponding with the Josetta Wilson bombing. It could be a coincidence, but Isabella left the clinic three days before the assassination and was back there bright and early the day after. Daphne left two days before and reported for duty the afternoon of the next day."

"I know I sound like a fussy mother, but keep reminding yourself these people are ruthless, however nice they appear. And that includes Daphne. Be careful, Denise."

It was only after I broke the connection I realized she had used my real name.

CHAPTER FOURTEEN

"Let's just chat," I said.

Rosemary looked at me with deep suspicion. "What about? You're not going to ask me how I feel, are you?"

I laughed. "It is a standard therapy line."

That actually got a faint smile on her surly face. "You've no idea how many times I've been asked that."

"Oh, I think I have," I said.

"So what are we going to talk about? My mother?"

"Not unless you want to."

"I bloody well don't!"

"Okay, how about this: Where do you see yourself five years from now?"

Rosemary frowned at me. "Five years from now? I've never thought about it."

"Humor me, and think about it."

"I'll be married to Graeme, and we'll have children."

"Describe your life."

Rosemary became quite animated, going into detailed accounts of her children—predictably a boy and a girl—and how she and Graeme would make a loving home. It was quite touching, and I was sorry she would soon have the shock of learning her Graeme was already married.

I wondered what kind of hell Thorwell was going through at the moment. If he told Fenella he was already married she'd be absolutely furious, and quite capable of punishing him by throwing him out of his clinics and ruining his professional standing. But if Thorwell kept quiet, what was he to do? Daphne had said she wouldn't divorce him, so he had only two alternatives: commit bigamy or stall the wedding as long as possible, hoping that Daphne would change her mind.

With a cold jolt I realized there was another alternative. He could have Daphne killed. But no—there was all that money hidden away in her name.

"What if you don't marry Graeme?" I said to Rosemary.

"I will," she said with perfect confidence. "My mother says so, and she always gets what she wants."

Fenella met me as I was leaving Rosemary's room. "If you do your job well, Dr. Sommers, you'll find me very generous. So far your interactions with my daughter are satisfactory." She put a pudgy hand on my arm. "And about that other matter . . . ?"

Obviously she was referring to her instruction to spy on Graeme Thorwell. "I believe there could be something," I said, suitably mysterious, "but may take a little time to get the details."

"I'll be here until next Sunday, when I must return to the States," said Fenella. "I'll expect a full report from you on Saturday, or earlier, if possible."

She didn't wait for my reply, but walked off, full of certainty that I would comply.

As I made my way to the secure unit, Lynda Lane caught up with me. With a sour smile, she said, "I saw you deep in conversation with Fenella van Berg. She's recruiting you as a secret agent, is she?"

"Why do you say that?"

"It's one of Fenella's charming little ways. She sets people to spy on each other. She's approached most of us at various times. Don't be sucked in. She's a bitch of the first order."

I'd been trusted with a keycard and the code for the secure unit, although I had to have someone else let me into the inner Sanctuary area. As I opened the door, Lynda said to me, "So what do you think of Graeme's pending marriage?"

The news was circulating already. "I'm not sure," I said vaguely. "I suppose it's a good thing."

Lynda Lane's long face was split with a huge grin. "Funniest thing I've heard for ages. It'll never happen, of course."

"No?"

"Would you want Fenella van Berg as you mother-in-law?"

"I don't suppose I would. But she does have an awful lot of money . . ."

"Money," said Lynda Lane. "It drives the world. It certainly drives *me*. Can't have too much of it, don't you agree? Soon Graeme won't have to worry about Fenella's fortune—he'll have one of his own."

As we entered the secure unit, Harry Gerlich came out of one of the rooms. "Lynda, a private word."

He took her aside for a moment, then nodded to me and went on his way.

"Pretentious prick," said Lynda Lane, scowling.

"What was all that about?" I asked, hoping that her animosity toward Gerlich would override her caution.

"Gerlich has this affectation—all his research subjects are programmed to speak his trademark phrase. Bloody stupid, if you ask me."

"But what's it for?" I asked, eyebrows raised. I was sure the words would be the ones uttered by both suicide bombers: *I am come to you.*

Lynda gave a cynical snort. "He's branding his product, that's what he says." Then, seeming to realize she'd revealed too much, she added quickly, "Forget I said anything about it. Gerlich doesn't like his business discussed."

I shrugged. "It's of no interest to me."

"Good. Keep it that way." She gave me a hard stare. "You wouldn't want to be on the wrong side of one of these doors, would you?

Without waiting for any response from me, Lynda Lane beckoned to one of the nurses, and together they went into one of the patient rooms.

I scarcely needed a reminder I was in a dangerous situation, but Lynda's veiled threat tightened my stomach. I was chilled by the images that rose in my imagination. I could see myself confined, drugged, with my senses scrambled, my will broken . . .

Giving myself a mental pull-yourself-together, I proceeded to the Sanctuary Project area where I was to have my daily session with Malcolm Ayres. I had to push a buzzer to gain entrance. I was startled when Daphne opened the door to me. "Hi," she said. Her smile was brief.

"What a pleasant surprise," I said. "I didn't expect to see you here. Are you to assist me with Malcolm Ayres?"

"Sorry, no, another patient. I'm waiting for Harry Gerlich."

"Verity Young?"

Daphne looked at me sharply. "You've been involved in her treatment?"

"Not at all. Dr. Gerlich merely showed me the patient when we were discussing the Sanctuary Project."

Daphne walked with me to Malcolm's room. Outside the door, she halted. Her expression was so serious I was prompted to say, "Is something wrong?"

She shook her head. "Not at all." Then she said, "Connie, sometimes people do things without thinking them through. It's only later, when you're in too deep, you have regrets."

"Regrets about what?"

She shook her head again. "We'll talk about it some other time."

Any chance I might have to persuade her to say more was lost when Gerlich appeared at the end of the corridor. I said to Daphne, "Tonight?"

"I'm on duty until late. Let's leave it I'll come to you, if I'm not too tired."

"Sounds good to me."

Gerlich, coming up to us, gave me a narrow look. "Is there some problem?"

"None at all," I said with a sunny smile.

He jerked his head at Daphne. "Come on. We can't waste time. We've a lot to do."

I looked after them as they disappeared into Verity Young's room. Daphne glanced back at me and raised her hand in a salute.

CHAPTER FIFTEEN

I slept badly. Daphne didn't come to me after her shift ended, and I was half glad that she hadn't. I worried that my objectivity, as far as she was concerned, was compromised.

After breakfast I went to the Sanctuary unit. "Where's Isabella this morning?" I asked the dour nurse who was preparing Malcolm for his session. I'd seen her around in the Sanctuary area, but had only spoken to her a couple of times. Her name was, improbably, Cherie Sweet. Her personality was at war with that appellation, as she was a hard-faced woman with a melancholy temperament.

"She's taking the rest of the week off. Some people have all the luck."

A shiver of alarm ran through me. This had been the pattern before the O'Neven bombing.

"Really? I'm a bit surprised. She never mentioned taking time off to me."

Cherie grunted. "Why would she? Isabella comes and goes as she pleases." Her scowl deepened. "She's got it made."

"Why do you say that?"

"She does what she likes. It's people like me who keep things running, while the Isabellas of the world swan around enjoying themselves."

Hoping this bitterness would make her talkative, I said, "Do you know where she's gone?"

That got me a narrow look. "I mind my own business."

"Wise move," I said. "Curiosity killed the cat, and all that."

I was impatient to get through the session with Malcolm and find out if Verity Young was still in the section. It was clear she was much more advanced in preparation than Malcolm was, so if she had disappeared too, then preparations for the next murder were well under way.

Gerlich's instruction to me today was to leave Malcolm in a deep trance at the close of the session. He would be timed to see how long it took for him to lapse into natural sleep.

I found it extraordinary that after only two prior sessions, Malcolm spontaneously fell into a light trance as soon as I spoke to him. It was as though I'd suddenly been given some strange, eerie power to take people's consciousness away from them.

"You want this paraphernalia turned on?" asked Cherie with a nod toward the sound and light systems I'd asked to be set up for the session.

"Yes, please."

I felt like I had my own private disco, but no one was dancing, certainly not Cherie, who clearly found the whole business an unnecessary nuisance. The bass rhythm and pulsing lights put Malcolm into a very deep trance almost immediately. In fact, the combination was so intrinsically mesmerizing I felt I had to spend some time outside the room to avoid going into a trance myself.

Leaving Cherie to observe the patient—I had a feeling no combination of rhythm and light would get to her—I took a break. There was no one in the corridor as I casually strolled to the sitting room at the end. That, too, was deserted. On my way back to Room Three and Malcolm, I stopped by Room Five and slid the peephole shutter open. The room was empty.

The moment I could get away, I sped to the administration office and, hiding my urgency, chatted with Teena. Phoebe came out of her office, nodded to me, then hurried off on some important mission.

Teena said with an unsympathetic grin, "Poor Phoebe. Fenella van Berg is keeping her hopping. Fenella wants this, she wants that. No delay, straight away. And this morning she was unhappy with breakfast, and has told Phoebe to arrange to have her New York chef flown in."

"You're kidding me."

Teena looked delighted. "I'm not. And Graeme's beside himself, what with Rosemary and all."

Even in my anxiety, I had to admire the gossip system in this place. "Does everyone know?"

"About the pending engagement? Oh, yes!"

We discussed Rosemary and Graeme's prospective union for a few minutes, and then I managed to turn the conversation to Isabella by saying in a confidential tone, "Cherie Sweet's been bending my ear about Isabella Nelson."

"Really?" said Teena, leaning forward in her wheelchair. "What's she been saying?"

"To begin with, she's upset about Isabella suddenly taking this week off."

"Oh, that's just Cherie," said Teena with an indulgent smile. "Isabella's not on holiday, she's accompanying a patient to another facility."

"Is she?" My expression invited confidences, and Teena, bless her, did not disappoint.

"A young schizophrenic girl from the secure unit." She shook her head. "It's tragic, isn't it, to have someone still at the beginning of her life afflicted with mental illness?"

"Awful," I agreed. Conveniently skating over the fact I'd been at Easehaven less than a week, I went on, "I've been working with Malcolm Ayres in that unit, so I've had a chance to get to know the other patients."

"I'm not sure of her name . . ." Teena swung her chair around and rustled through a pile of papers on her desk. "Yes, here it is. Verity Young. Her parents requested she be moved to a clinic nearer their home. Isabella's escorting Verity there and helping to settle her in."

I glanced at the form she was showing me. The information on it had to be false, but I automatically memorized the details anyway. "Heavens, Teena," I said, "fancy taking this young woman away from Easehaven. I can't imagine she'd get better treatment anywhere else."

We both shook our heads over this imponderable action. My skin prickled as I introduced my next question. "I need to discuss some patient details with Daphne. Would you check her schedule and see where she is, please?"

Teena helpfully pulled up Daphne's schedule on her computer monitor. "That's funny," she said. "Daphne should be on duty now, but her place has been taken by Joyce Parsons. Do you want me to check why?"

I shrugged. "If you wouldn't mind."

"Zena, code red."

"Activated." All available intelligence resources would be diverted to foiling the possible assassination attempt.

I had no time for a stroll outside, and called from my bathroom, where I had the water gushing into the basin to cover my words just in case the place was bugged.

I went rapidly through the information I had. Accompanied by Isabella Nelson, Verity Young had been whisked away from Easehaven very early this morning. Daphne Webster had left shortly afterwards, with the excuse that she had an unexpected family emergency. Graeme Thorwell and Harry Gerlich were still here on site. So was Lynda Lane.

"Maybe Daphne's family emergency is genuine," I said hopefully.

"I'll check and get back to you. Sit tight, Connie, but be prepared to go if I give the word. You're the only one who can identify Verity Young."

"The photos you have of Isabella Nelson show her with red hair. Now she's dyed it brown."

"Okay, got that. What about Daphne Webster?"

I made myself sound matter-of-fact. "Last time I saw her, Daphne Webster hadn't changed her appearance."

"Here's what we have at the moment," said Zena. "Henders has his next scheduled public appearance on Friday afternoon in Sydney. We'll try to persuade him to be a no show at the last moment, so we can put a security cordon around the venue and carry out a person-to-person search. We're assuming this will be another assassination by suicide bomber, but that's not the only possibility, so we'll have hazard teams in place."

I'd had time to imagine any number of nightmare scenarios. I said, "I'm sure you've considered the possibility that Isabella realizes what's happening, and to create a diversion, detonates by remote control the bomb Verity's wearing."

"We've considered that, but what makes you think it has to be Isabella with the remote trigger? Couldn't it just as easily be Daphne Webster?"

"Of course it could," I said, not wanting to believe it.

CHAPTER SIXTEEN

The rest of Tuesday, Wednesday and Thursday passed slowly with me alternately wanting Friday to come and dreading the death and destruction it might bring. I continued my role as psychotherapist without being revealed as a fraud, and in Rosemary Lloyd's case I came to believe I was actually doing some good. I only tried to induce light trances a couple of times. Mostly I just prompted Rosemary to discuss her life and hopes for the future.

Fenella took me aside to say approvingly, "Rosemary's opening up to you, Dr. Sommers. You seem to be the friend she's always needed—someone with no hidden agenda. The children of the rich have a hard row to hoe. So many people try to take advantage."

Zena reported back on Daphne's excuse of having a family emergency. It wasn't true. "I thought so," I said, flooded with disappointment and regret. Daphne had to be implicated, I'd come to accept that, but now it looked like she was an active player in the conspiracy.

I saw Henders' fleshy, self-satisfied face on the television screen a couple of times, and dreamed about him the few short hours I managed to sleep on Thursday night. All efforts to trace Verity, Isabella and Daphne had failed, so I was to be picked up by Joe Ibbotson at a rendezvous point three kilometers down the coast and taken to the venue where Henders would appear in the late afternoon.

A network of surveillance cameras had been set up at every entrance to the auditorium, the images from them feeding into a bank of monitors in the basement. Guards at security gates would be slowing the admission of the public so there'd be time to scan for individual faces. I was the only one who could reliably identify Verity Young, so my presence was essential.

"Why's Ibbotson picking me up?" I'd demanded of Zena.

"It's a joint ASIO-CIA operation. He had the seniority to insist."

"Should I be flattered?"

"He's spoken very highly of you." She added teasingly, "Besides, you know we're always being told how important cooperation is between our two great countries."

First thing on Friday morning I went to Phoebe's office. "Phoebe, I've just had some very upsetting news."

This was guaranteed to catch her attention. "You have?" she said, clearly keen for a tidbit to add to the day's gossip quotient.

"One of my closest friends in Sydney has had a dreadful car accident. Drunken driver ran a red light and ploughed into her car."

"How awful! Anyone else hurt?"

I resisted the temptation to increase the cast by adding fictional children, and said, "No, just Megan. The guy that hit her was hardly scratched."

"Tsk! Isn't it always the way?"

"I've got to go to her, Phoebe. I'll be back this evening. I'm so sorry to land you with this change of schedule . . ." I gave her a piteous expression.

"Go, go," she said. "Don't give a thought to it. I'll look after everything."

I thanked her, murmured something about a friend in need to Teena on the way out, and, looking suitably worried, rushed off to my car.

The rendezvous point was an abandoned petrol station off the main road. I found it without difficulty and parked my car out of sight inside a repair bay. Outside, next to the abandoned pumps, an anonymous dark sedan was waiting. Joe Ibbotson jumped out as I approached.

"Constance! It's great to see you." He looked me up and down approvingly. I was wearing a loose blue top, navy slacks and flat shoes. If anything physical happened, I was dressed for action. Nodding, he said, "Looking good. Looking good."

"How's your rescued agent?"

Ibbotson's smile faded. "It's going slowly. They really fried her brains. Should eventually recover, though." His eyes narrowed. "I can't wait to nail the bastards."

"Let's do it." I sounded gung-ho, but inwardly I was quaking. Trying to prevent a suicide bomber from detonating the charge had frequently resulted in a premature blast and the death of the person intervening. And there was a good chance I'd be that person.

Ibbotson opened the front passenger door for me. "My buddy can ride in the back."

The buddy turned out to be another CIA operative, Arnie Ash, who grinned at me and said, "Joe drives like a bat out of hell. I don't mind being in the back seat."

Ibbotson said into his phone, "Pickup made. We're underway." Shoving it back into his pocket, he said, "Arnie's got a present for you."

Ash passed over a subcompact Glock. "Zena said it was your favorite," he said. "And here's a waist holster."

"Okay," said Ibbotson, stamping on the accelerator, "let's get this show on the road."

Ash had been accurate. Ibbotson drove like one demented. I expected any moment to have the cops pull us over, but we screamed down the Sydney-Newcastle Freeway without incident, making the outskirts of Sydney in record time. When we hit surface roads, however, blaring horns, squealing brakes and purple language from other motorists became the order of the day.

Ash kept reporting our progress into his phone, or peering at its tiny screen for text messages. We were on the Pacific Highway at Killara when he read a text message and said, "Ah, shit! Slight change of plans. Henders is calling one of his stupid flash meetings . . . what does he call them? Yeah, spontaneous clusters. Well, he's used email and messaging to get one underway at a big shopping mall."

He punched in a number, which was answered immediately. "Yeah? Shit! He's definitely going ahead with it? Where? Hold it." Ash flipped through a street directory, swearing softly under his breath. "I've got the location. Which entrance?" His finger stabbed at the map. "Right, we're on our way."

"Where to?" asked Ibbotson, grinning fiercely. He was obviously having a good time.

It had been decided to divert us to the spur-of-the-moment meeting as a precaution. Security teams were leaving the auditorium to join us at the mall as soon as possible. If, as expected, this was a false alarm, we would regroup at the scheduled venue in the city.

Ash was an excellent navigator. Following his instructions, Ibbotson careened off the highway, hurtled down side streets and onto another main road. We rocketed through intersections, our driver apparently oblivious to whether the traffic lights were green or red. When I was thoroughly lost, Ash said triumphantly, "And here we are!"

It was a standard shopping mall surrounded by a sea of cars, its bulky buildings apparently designed by the same uninspired architects responsible for a thousand other depressingly similar centers.

Ibbotson scattered pedestrians as he zoomed through the car park, screeching to a stop in a handicapped parking zone near the main entrance.

"Find Henders and stop him from appearing, no matter what he says," Ibbotson barked at Ash. To me he said, "Let's go get 'em."

Ibbotson and I hurried into the mall. We didn't run—that would get us too much attention. I checked my Glock, snuggled in a holster and hidden by my loose top. I was a fair shot, but firing in a crowded situation like this would be a last resort.

We'd had a quick discussion in the car about whether to try clearing the mall with a bogus fire alarm, but as it was a long shot that the attempt on Henders' life would be made at this unscheduled meeting—the conspirators presumably would have had little time to prepare—it was decided not to risk the potential for panic and injury.

Bright, full-of-energy shopping music almost drowned out the loud hum of many people all talking at the same time. I groaned when I saw where the crowd was coalescing, some waving signs with Henders' face and name. Any meaningful security was impossible. There was a permanent metal stage set up in an assembly area in the middle of the mall. Nearby, escalators ferried people to and from the upper floors. Mall guards had obviously been alerted, and were stationed top and bottom, but they were allowing everyone to travel up and down without hindrance.

On the side of the stage furthest from us was a large fish pool with water lilies. In the center of the pool a small fountain cascaded bilious green water. Behind that again was an area filled with benches full of individuals resting weary feet.

There seemed to be thousands in the mall: shoppers laden with bags, curious onlookers, mothers with wailing kids, plus the many people who'd specifically come to see Henders in the flesh. Members of a television crew, sweating, arrived at a quick trot and muscled their way to a good vantage point.

I scanned the faces, hoping, yet dreading, to see familiar features. Was Verity Young here, a bomb strapped to her slight body, waiting

159

to send Henders to oblivion? If so, only Ibbotson and I were present to stop the atrocity. I hoped Ash had been successful in at least slowing Henders down. The longer things were delayed, the more time it gave our reinforcements to arrive.

I'd just about decided this was all a waste of time, when I saw her.

"Joe!" I said in a fierce whisper.

"What?"

"There, way over on the other side. The woman in the gray dress near the escalator. It's Isabella Nelson."

"The fat, middle-aged one carrying the big tapestry handbag?"

"She wouldn't thank you for that description, but yes."

He gave my shoulder a quick squeeze. "I'm on it. She won't detonate that bomb. I'll die first."

Looking into his thin, intense face, I believed him. All the irritation he had caused me in the past melted away. "Joe Ibbotson, you're all right."

"We need Verity," he said.

"She'll be near the stage." We parted, Ibbotson speaking into his phone to advise we had a positive sighting as he unobtrusively made his way toward Isabella. I set out to get to the front of the rapidly thickening mob waiting for a glimpse of Henders, their bright new political savior.

Nearer to the stage, the crowd was thicker and less amenable to my attempts to get through. "Watch it, girly," snarled one thick-necked guy, shoving me hard.

I desperately scanned for Verity. She could be wearing her long brown hair up. She could be disguised with a wig. I might be a couple of meters from her, and never know.

A hum was generated from the front. "Henders! Henders!" A bunch of people near me whipped out placards, each with a letter of Henders' name, and waved them madly for the TV cameras.

Henders appeared on the descending escalator to rising applause. He was followed by a fat guy I took to be the ineffectual bodyguard,

160

and then Arnie Ash. It was clear Ash had not been persuasive enough to stop the appearance.

The sound system crackled and the bouncy music faded away. Henders waved as he slowly descended on the escalator. "Good on you mate!" shrieked someone near me.

Henders would be Verity's magnet. If she followed the script, she'd embrace him, saying, "I am come to you," before she blew herself up. Not much of a window of opportunity for me, but better than nothing.

If I could get to Henders, I knew Verity would be close by. But getting close to Henders was easier said than done. No one wanted to let me through. The crowd at the front was a solid mass of bodies, most chanting, "Henders! Henders!"

I put my head down and wriggled through gaps, stamped on feet, elbowed ribs. Someone hit me with a glancing blow. "Who do you think you are, you bitch?"

Henders mounted the few shallow metal steps to the stage just as I reached the front of the crowd. His bodyguard had stopped at the bottom of the escalator, and was chatting to someone.

A roar of approval rose behind me as Henders raised both fists in the air.

And there she was!

CHAPTER SEVENTEEN

Verity Young, brown hair flowing to her shoulders, her eyes wide, stared at Henders with absolute concentration. She was about three meters away from me, and before I could get to her she'd made the steps and climbed onto the stage.

Henders noticed her with a smile. I heard him say, "Hello, darlin', and what can I do for you?"

The Glock in my hand, I scrambled onto the stage. Henders, astonished, yelled at me, "Hey, what are you doing?"

I was focused intensely on Verity. She was smiling beatifically at Henders. I had a split second to decide what action to take. Her right hand was concealed. That meant she had her finger on the trigger. If I wrestled with her, she could activate the device before I could stop her. A gunshot might detonate the bomb.

I don't believe she even registered I was there on the stage. As she stepped forward, her gaze fixed on Henders, opening her mouth to deliver the words so cruelly taught, I reached her.

The blow was just below the point of her chin, the heel of my hand snapping her head back with such force that she fell backward as if her feet had been swept from under her. The sharp crack as her head hit the metal stage was sickening.

I fell to my knees, ready to strike her again, but she lay inert, unconscious.

Henders grabbed at my shoulder. "What the hell!"

"She's wearing a bomb."

"A bomb!" His expression almost comically panicked, he scuttled backwards until he fell off the edge of the stage in an undignified flurry of arms and legs.

A woman shrieked, "A bomb! There's a bomb!" As others echoed the cry, pandemonium broke out as those in the front frantically tried to distance themselves from the threat.

As the crowd thinned, I saw someone moving purposefully toward the stage. A woman in jeans with a denim shirt and a shoulder bag. My heart jumped as I recognized Daphne.

I stood up. She halted in shocked surprise. Our eyes locked. I was too far away to hear, but I saw her say, "Connie?"

At my feet, Verity Young groaned.

Still staring at me, Daphne fumbled with her bag. The stinging realization that it was Daphne who had the remote trigger hit me like a blow.

Time seemed to stretch. As though in slow motion, I swung the Glock up until the sights were steady on her face. A head shot was my only chance. She had to be instantly executed, not wounded. Even if mortally hurt, she could still activate the bomb, and blow Verity and me to bloody pieces.

"Oh, Daphne," I whispered, my finger tightening. I knew at that instant I could kill her, no matter what the cost to me, as mercilessly as she had planned to kill others.

Before I could fire, Ibbotson hit her from behind. Daphne stumbled forward, fell on hands and knees. She scrabbled for the bag. He stamped hard on her fingers. Tearing the bag away from her, he shoved his gun in her face. I saw his lips move as he said something.

Arnie Ash arrived at a run, followed by uniformed cops and white-coated medics. "The reinforcements arrive, just when all the fun is over," he said to me. He looked down at Verity Young. "The bomb squad's on its way."

"Where's Isabella?"

"Under guard and mighty unhappy."

"She didn't have the remote," I said.

Ash looked at me, surprised. "She did."

Ibbotson came jogging over to us, a broad smile on his face. In one hand he held Daphne's shoulder bag. He gingerly removed something resembling the device used for opening garage doors. "That was a near thing."

"Nearer than you think," said Ash. "Isabella Nelson had one too."

Ibbotson turned to look at Daphne, who was on her feet, hand-cuffed, a uniformed officer on either side. "Well, I'll be," he said, quite admiring. "A backup for a backup."

Daphne lifted her chin and stared at me. I stared back. She dropped her gaze first. I said to Ibbotson, "What did you say to her when you shoved your gun in her face?"

Amazingly, Ibbotson reddened. "Do I have to say?"

"You do."

With an embarrassed smile, he said, "I told her, 'You mess with Connie, you mess with me.'"

"Aw shucks," I said.

CHAPTER EIGHTEEN

I never saw Easehaven again.

Constance Sommers vanished, as if she'd never existed. Someone from ASIO packed up the things in my room and wiped surfaces clean of fingerprints. My personnel file was removed from the clinic computer. Someone else picked up my rental car and returned it to the company. And because my face could never be shown in the media, despite vehement protests, the television crew who'd been at the mall found their material seized for national security reasons.

Within minutes of the attempt on Henders' life, a squad of Federal Police had descended on the clinic, throwing a cordon around Easehaven even Fenella van Berg with all her money and influence could not penetrate.

Everyone was detained while intelligence agents and law enforcement sifted through the evidence and took copious statements. Graeme Thorwell, Harry Gerlich and Isabella Nelson were arrested and charged with the murder of Norah Bradley, who had unwisely tried to blackmail Gerlich for a larger slice of the pie. The killing, by fatal injection, had been carried out by Isabella at Gerlich's instigation. Graeme Thorwell, with great reluctance, had helped dispose of the body.

The same three, plus Lynda Lane and Daphne Webster, were charged with the attempted murder of Henders. Other charges related to kidnapping, false imprisonment and torture were pending.

Phoebe Murdoch and the rest of the staff were exonerated, although Cherie Sweet was to be called before a disciplinary board and was likely to lose her nursing credentials.

Earle was arrested in New Zealand for conspiracy to murder his ex-partner. Douglas Wilton, who had paid to have the Kerns killed in a head-on collision, was arrested as he tried to flee Australia. In the States, a political rival of Senator O'Neven's was indicted. Arrests were made in Britain and France for other suicide killings orchestrated by the Easehaven murder team, and requests to extradite Thorwell and Gerlich were about to be filed.

"What's happening with Fenella and Rosemary?" I asked Cynthia, who was Zena no more. We were sitting in her neat office in Canberra at ASIO headquarters, where I'd been undergoing the usual post-assignment debriefing.

Cynthia shrugged. "No charges, of course. Neither of them knew anything about the Sanctuary Project."

"I didn't mean that. How's Rosemary handling the fact her Graeme is a murderer?"

"As well as can be expected, which is, as you won't be surprised to learn, not very well. Perhaps that's why her mother is keeping the three clinics open, and is auditioning for a new medical director." Cynthia smiled her charming angular smile. "I have a feeling whoever the lucky man is, he'll find he has a rather demanding role to play in Rosemary's life."

"I feel sorry for her," I said. "Rosemary, that is, not Fenella."

"Fenella van Berg speaks very highly of Constance Sommers. In fact, she asked if she could see you again to discuss her daughter. She wasn't pleased to be told it was impossible."

"I did get rather adept at hypnotizing people," I said smugly.

"Oh, yes?"

Irked by her amusement, I said, "A challenge, Cynthia. Let me have a go at hypnotizing you."

She cocked her head and gave me a long, considering look. "All right, if you like."

"You will?" Frankly, I was astonished, but happy to play along.

I arranged her comfortably in a chair and started my routine. It all went smoothly. Cynthia closed her eyes and her breathing deepened.

"You are under my power," I said, "and will hear only my voice."

I was pretty sure she was faking it, but hey, why not give it a go?

"You feel relaxed, peaceful. You will answer my questions fully and freely. You will tell me all you think and feel about Denise Cleever."

Cynthia opened one eye.

"I don't think so," she said.

Publications from
BELLA BOOKS, INC.
The best in contemporary lesbian fiction

P.O. Box 10543, Tallahassee, FL 32302
Phone: 800-729-4992
www.bellabooks.com

DEATH BY DEATH by Claire McNab. 167 pp. 5th Denise
Cleever Thriller.   ISBN 1-931513-34-1 $12.95

CAUGHT IN THE NET by Jessica Thomas. 188 pp. A Wickedly observant story of mystery, danger and love in Provincetown.   ISBN
1-931513-54-6 $12.95

DREAMS FOUND by Lyn Denison. 201 pp. Australian Riley embarks
on a journey to meet her birth mother . . . and gains not just a family, but
the love of her life.   ISBN 1-931513-58-9 $12.95

A MOMENT'S INDISCRETION by Peggy J. Herring.
Jackie is torn between her better judgment and the overwhelming attrac-
tion she feels for Valerie.   ISBN# 1-931513-59-7 $12.95

IN EVERY PORT by Karin Kallmaker. 224 pp. Jessica's sexy,
adventuresome travels.   ISBN 1-931513-36-8 $12.95

TOUCHWOOD by Karin Kallmaker. 240 pp. Loving
May/December romance.   ISBN 1-931513-37-6 $12.95

WATERMARK by Karin Kallmaker. 248 pp. One burning
question . . . how to lead her back to love? ISBN 1-931513-38-4 $12.95

EMBRACE IN MOTION by Karin Kallmaker. 240 pp. A
whirlwind love affair.   ISBN 1-931513-39-2 $12.95

ONE DEGREE OF SEPARATION by Karin Kallmaker. 232 pp.
Can an Iowa City librarian find love and passion when a California
girl surfs into the close-knit Dyke Capital of the Midwest?
                                        ISBN 1-931513-30-9 $12.95

CRY HAVOC A Detective Franco Mystery by Baxter Clare. 240 pp.
A dead hustler with a headless rooster in his lap sends Lt. L.A.
Franco headfirst against Mother Love.   ISBN 1-931513931-7 $12.95

DISTANT THUNDER by Peggy J. Herring. 294 pp. Bankrobbing drifter Cordy awakens strange new feelings in Leo in this romantic tale set in the old West. ISBN 1-931513-28-7 $12.95

COP OUT by Claire McNab. 216 pp. 4th Detective Inspector Carol Ashton Mystery. ISBN 1-931513-29-5 $12.95

BLOOD LINK by Claire McNab. 159 pp. 15th Detective Inspector Carol Ashton Mystery. Is Carol unwittingly playing into a deadly plan? ISBN 1-931513-27-9 $12.95

TALK OF THE TOWN by Saxon Bennett. 239 pp. With enough beer, barbecue and B.S., anything is possible! ISBN 1-931513-18-X $12.95

MAYBE NEXT TIME by Karin Kallmaker. 256 pp. Sabrina Starling has it all: fame, money, women—and pain. Nothing hurts like the one that got away. ISBN 1-931513-26-0 $12.95

WHEN GOOD GIRLS GO BAD: A Motor City Thriller by Therese Szymanski. 230 pp. Brett, Randi, and Allie join forces to stop a serial killer. ISBN 1-931513-11-2 12.95

A DAY TOO LONG: A Helen Black Mystery by Pat Welch. 328 pp. This time Helen's fate is in her own hands. ISBN 1-931513-22-8 $12.95

THE RED LINE OF YARMALD by Diana Rivers. 256 pp. The Hadra's only hope lies in a magical red line . . . Climactic sequel to *Clouds of War*. ISBN 1-931513-23-6 $12.95

OUTSIDE THE FLOCK by Jackie Calhoun. 224 pp. Jo embraces her new love and life. ISBN 1-931513-13-9 $12.95

LEGACY OF LOVE by Marianne K. Martin. 224 pp. Read the whole Sage Bristo story. ISBN 1-931513-15-5 $12.95

STREET RULES: A Detective Franco Mystery by Baxter Clare. 304 pp. Gritty, fast-paced mystery with compelling Detective L.A. Franco ISBN 1-931513-14-7 $12.95

RECOGNITION FACTOR: 4th Denise Cleever Thriller by Claire McNab. 176 pp. Denise Cleever tracks a notorious terrorist to America. ISBN 1-931513-24-4 $12.95

NORA AND LIZ by Nancy Garden. 296 pp. Lesbian romance by the author of *Annie on My Mind*. ISBN 1931513-20-1 $12.95

MIDAS TOUCH by Frankie J. Jones. 208 pp. Sandra had everything but love. ISBN 1-931513-21-X $12.95

BEYOND ALL REASON by Peggy J. Herring. 240 pp. A romance hotter than Texas. ISBN 1-9513-25-2 $12.95

ACCIDENTAL MURDER: 14th Detective Inspector Carol Ashton Mystery by Claire McNab. 208 pp. Carol Ashton tracks an elusive killer. ISBN 1-931513-16-3 $12.95

SEEDS OF FIRE: Tunnel of Light Trilogy, Book 2 by Karin Kallmaker writing as Laura Adams. 274 pp. Intriguing sequel to *Sleight of Hand*. ISBN 1-931513-19-8 $12.95

DRIFTING AT THE BOTTOM OF THE WORLD by Auden Bailey. 288 pp. Beautifully written first novel set in Antarctica. ISBN 1-931513-17-1 $12.95

CLOUDS OF WAR by Diana Rivers. 288 pp. Women unite to defend Zelindar! ISBN 1-931513-12-0 $12.95

DEATHS OF JOCASTA: 2nd Micky Knight Mystery by J.M. Redmann. 408 pp. Sexy and intriguing Lambda Literary Award-nominated mystery. ISBN 1-931513-10-4 $12.95

LOVE IN THE BALANCE by Marianne K. Martin. 256 pp. The classic lesbian love story, back in print! ISBN 1-931513-08-2 $12.95

THE COMFORT OF STRANGERS by Peggy J. Herring. 272 pp. Lela's work was her passion . . . until now. ISBN 1-931513-09-0 $12.95

CHICKEN by Paula Martinac. 208 pp. Lynn finds that the only thing harder than being in a lesbian relationship is ending one. ISBN 1-931513-07-4 $11.95

TAMARACK CREEK by Jackie Calhoun. 208 pp. An intriguing story of love and danger. ISBN 1-931513-06-6 $11.95

DEATH BY THE RIVERSIDE: 1st Micky Knight Mystery by J.M. Redmann. 320 pp. Finally back in print, the book that launched the Lambda Literary Award-winning Micky Knight mystery series. ISBN 1-931513-05-8 $11.95

EIGHTH DAY: A Cassidy James Mystery by Kate Calloway. 272 pp. In the eighth installment of the Cassidy James mystery series, Cassidy goes undercover at a camp for troubled teens. ISBN 1-931513-04-X $11.95

MIRRORS by Marianne K. Martin. 208 pp. Jean Carson and Shayna Bradley fight for a future together. ISBN 1-931513-02-3 $11.95

THE ULTIMATE EXIT STRATEGY: A Virginia Kelly Mystery by Nikki Baker. 240 pp. The long-awaited return of the wickedly observant Virginia Kelly. ISBN 1-931513-03-1 $11.95